# DELAYED REACTION

In support of

The
ROYAL
MARSDEN
*Cancer Charity*

# DELAYED REACTION

An unscheduled stop sets in motion
a dramatic train of events...

Self-published by Just Write, Amersham

First published in Great Britain 2015

Collection © Just Write 2015

All rights reserved

ISBN 978-0-9931222-2-4

Design and artwork by Oliver Payne and Stuart Tennant.

Printed and bound in Great Britain.

A share of the profits from the sale of each copy will be donated to The Royal Marsden Hospital (Registered Charity Number 1095197).

Just Write is RMCC supporter number 240434.

*For Sally Norton, who made the whole thing possible.*

# INTRODUCTION

When I set up my own creative writing class in Amersham just over three years ago, I never imagined it would lead to this – writing the introduction to a second book of short stories from the award-winning writers in my class; award-winning writers who have become my friends.

The group has had an amazing year. They've celebrated winning the Best Anthology Award from *Writing Magazine* for their first book *Spilling the Beans*, and they've handed over a cheque for £1,000 to The Royal Marsden Cancer Charity. And, of course, they've written another book, the one you have in your hands now.

This new collection of ten short stories will appeal to anyone who has ever sat on a train and wondered about the person sitting opposite them, guessing what they do and wondering what's going on in their life. What's really special is that, while each story can be enjoyed alone, they have actually been designed to work together as a cohesive whole. It's a brilliant idea and I really think the writers have pulled it off.

To the outside world, the Just Write group makes creating a new book look easy, but I know there's been a huge amount of work going on behind the scenes. There's been writing, rewriting, proofreading and designing – there's even been a train trip along the route to check key details are correct. While they've done all this, they've held down jobs, cared for families and, rather wonderfully, welcomed a new grandchild.

You're in for a treat with *Delayed Reaction* and I really hope you enjoy reading it as much as I have.

**Sally Norton**

This is the second set of short stories which are the direct result of Sally Norton's decision to run a creative writing class in Amersham. The authors, all members of that group, decided to meet and write during the long summer breaks. Their first book, *Spilling the Beans*, won *Writing Magazine's* Writers' Circle Anthology Award for 2014. The citation said, in part, "With a canny approach to writing a collaborative anthology, Buckinghamshire group Just Write create a seamless fictional world in *Spilling the Beans*."

Their £250 prize was added to sales income and, in August 2015, the group presented a cheque for £1,000 to The Royal Marsden Cancer Charity towards the purchase of a room steriliser. This piece of equipment allows a room to be sterilised by ultraviolet light in a few minutes, a task that would otherwise take many days' manual labour: speeding up the cleaning allows more patients to be treated.

*Lesley Close on the right, hands a cheque to Sara Lister (Head of Pastoral Care) of The Royal Marsden while David Matthews, now in remission, holds a promotional copy of 'Spilling the Beans' at the Just Write summer barbecue August 2015.*

# DAVID'S STORY, PART 2

Just Write was inspired to support The Royal Marsden Cancer Charity by the close association of one of our writers with David Matthews, a young man of 23 who was diagnosed with Stage 4 Ewing's Sarcoma in July 2014. We are delighted to report that, thanks to nine months of intensive and gruelling chemo and radiotherapy at The Royal Marsden Hospital, David is now cancer-free. Much of the equipment and additional facilities in the Children and Young Persons' Unit, where David was treated, was purchased by The Royal Marsden Cancer Charity as NHS funding will not stretch to the many extras which make life bearable for young cancer sufferers.

"The Royal Marsden Hospital saved my life," David writes. "I spent weeks in hospital, and benefited from the extras bought by the charity which made the place feel more like home – not to mention the state of the art scanners and other equipment. Thank you for buying this book so we can build on the £1,000 already raised for this amazing charity through sales of Just Write's first book of short stories."

# DEDICATION

*Dedicated to The Royal Marsden Hospital, for the wonderful work they do.*

In support of

## About The Royal Marsden Cancer Charity

Every year The Royal Marsden provides treatment and care for more than 50,000 cancer patients and is at the forefront of cancer research. Its work influences how all cancer patients are treated and cared for, not just in its own hospitals but all over the world.

With the help of The Royal Marsden Cancer Charity, The Royal Marsden can continue to push the boundaries and benefit cancer patients, wherever they are.

The Royal Marsden Cancer Charity raises money to help The Royal Marsden provide world-class diagnosis, treatment and care for cancer patients, and supports the hospital's pioneering work in cancer research.

By supporting The Royal Marsden in this way the charity aims to make life better for people with cancer everywhere and strive for a future without it.

# Acknowledgements

Lesley Close edited the texts and she would like to acknowledge the help she received from Debbie Hunter. Lesley would also like to acknowledge the generous technical assistance she was given by John Wesley. Any technical errors to do with signalling or train driving matters are down to her need for a degree of literary licence rather than faulty information.

Stuart Tennant and Oliver Payne worked tirelessly on the design and layout of the book, and the authors' grateful thanks are due to them.

Above all, thanks are due to the authors who wrote the stories, Janet Mears for her superb proofreading (any remaining mistakes are the fault of the editor, not Janet), and the many anonymous 'test' readers whose input improved the stories immensely.

# Contents

# Nemesis
## by Liz Losty

GEORGIE finished her last email, then double-checked she had saved the changes on her monthly report before powering off her laptop. She slipped it back into her bag and gave a small sigh of relief as she stowed it under her seat. She had finally caught up on her workload and was glad to switch off, finish work for the day and enjoy the journey. Now she was free to focus on giving Mum and Tom all her time and attention when she arrived.

It felt good to be going back home, albeit for only one night. She really needed to see them both to reassure herself that they were coping. Tom hadn't been well and was just out of hospital after another heart episode. This time the doctors had finally done something and inserted stents. It had sounded scary but her mother told her the specialists were confident that Tom would feel a huge improvement. Georgie hoped so, for his sake and for her mother's. She thought about them both and how much she worried about them now – not so long ago it was them worrying about her.

But she had resolved in her mind that they would be fine. She would make sure of it, whether it was paying for private health care or seeing the best specialists. Maybe even a nice weekend away to spoil them, but only if they felt up to it. They deserved to be happy together for as long as possible, and she owed them so much after all that she had put them through. The sweetest thing about them was that they never brought it up; they never seemed to dwell on it or hold a grudge. They had all, by wordless agreement, left the bad times in the past. The most they had ever said about the matter was when they chatted with friends about the trials of parenthood: "Teenagers . . . don't talk to us about teenagers, eh Georgie?" Even that was done with good humour and with a kind, knowing smile that only they shared.

She thought back to Mum and Tom's wedding day, seven years ago. Mum had looked so beautiful and, somehow, so young, dressed in a soft cream silk dress with a stylish wide-brimmed hat. With her shy smile she looked so demure, blushing at all the attention and yet radiant because of it. And Tom had been fit to burst with pride when he saw her. His wedding speech had said it all, not maudlin or soppy – just heartfelt. Two people who had both loved and lost and who had finally found solace in each other when they thought they would never have the chance to love again. When Tom raised his glass of champagne and asked everyone to toast his beautiful bride, it was with the words 'Grow old with me: the best is yet to come'.

Georgie smiled as she remembered how Mum and Tom had looked at each other when he said that, and how relieved she was to see her mum truly happy again.

Georgie stared out of the carriage window, lost in memories, her mind wandering through times past as the train travelled through the landscape; lone houses, narrow roads and rolling green fields. The long green hedgerows stood out like straight, neat seams that knitted the fields and countryside together into one huge quilt. Georgie smiled to herself. It was strange that, despite everything that had happened in the past, she still enjoyed travelling by train. She found it almost hypnotic to tune into the rhythm of the train as it sped north.

Her favourite game as a child on long train journeys had been to look out of the window and imagine she was in two places at once. The sad Georgie was stuck on the train looking out and the happy Georgie was outside, laughing, reckless and brave, riding a strong black horse and galloping madly alongside the train, wearing a long white gypsy dress with her waves of golden hair flowing behind. She could sit transfixed for hours as she conjured up this image, not wanting to be interrupted for fear of breaking the spell. She would imagine the happy Georgie thundering along on the sleek-coated horse, anticipating every fence and hedge and encouraging it to jump them cleanly; the imaginary horse never broke its stride but raced along and kept up with the clattering train.

The happy Georgie was wild and free; she kept looking through the window at the sad, scared Georgie, willing her to smile. They were joined by an invisible thread, a telepathic urge to connect. When sad Georgie's mouth curved involuntarily into a gentle smile, brave Georgie knew her work was done and the spell was broken. The fantasy would vanish, the imaginary Georgie on her horse would fade away, and the real Georgie would turn away from the window to gaze around the carriage as if awakening from a dream.

She would look at her mother, sitting opposite, who always had a sad face unless it was over-laced by worry and that was worse. When she looked back on her childhood her mother always seemed sad, or depressed, or tearful. But the worst was when she didn't seem anything. It was almost as if her soul had left her and there was just this blank-faced, mute, exhausted shadow left; not her mother at all. It felt like that for a long time. The gnawing worry had been a constant in Georgie's life for years.

But if Georgie really concentrated and dug deep, she could remember earlier times and memories of when her mother had been happy. That was when her father was still alive and still at home. The one thing she knew for sure was that they loved each other. Not just because they hugged, or snuggled together on the sofa, or talked over each other in excitement, or sat silently in contentment, all of which Georgie had considered signs of love in her child's world. No: the real reason she knew they loved each other was that her father would make her mother laugh until tears ran down her face and she would bat him away with her hands, telling him to stop while he continued aping around and acting out his funny stories and jokes. Georgie would laugh too, although she didn't always understand the jokes: quite often her mother would say, "No, Steve, stop. Georgie can hear you." And they would both turn to her, laughing, and scoop her up: a *team hug*, her father used to call it. He was so tall and strong, with dark brown curly hair and deep blue eyes framed by long dark lashes. Her mother always said it wasn't fair that he got such lashes naturally while she had to spend a fortune on mascara to get anything like them, and they would laugh again. He was so handsome and, in Georgie's memory, always smiling.

Yet there were many gaps in her memories, and some things which she had deliberately blanked out in a desperate act of self-preservation. Sometimes it was too painful to revisit the bad times.

Georgie believed she must have been eight years old when her father was taken away from them. She had an abiding memory, which must have been from a few months before then, of going into her parents' room one morning while they were both still asleep. She crawled under the quilt at the bottom of the bed and wriggled her way up so that she could edge her way in and lie between them. Her mother opened a sleepy eye and mumbled her name before pulling her close into her warm and safe embrace. Georgie remembered turning and looking at her father's face and wondering if he was really asleep. She poked his chin, then his cheek, and finally drew up his eyelid to open the windows to his soul.

"Georgie . . . I'm trying to have a lie-in here," he scolded, but he smiled and pulled her into his arms. "I had her first," said her mother. Then began the most delightful tug of love, as they pulled her first one way then the other: it ended in tickles that left her giggling, breathless and giddy with delight.

"Calm down Steve. She'll have a coughing fit," said her mum, laughing at Georgie's red face.

"OK then. No more tickles, only kisses. So you choose – a butterfly kiss or an Eskimo kiss?" Georgie put her finger to her chin, feigning thoughtfulness, as she weighed up her choices.

"Butterfly kiss today, please Daddy," she announced.

Her father put his face against hers and fluttered his eyelids so that his eyelashes gently brushed and tickled the soft skin of Georgie's cheek. All three of them laughed and drifted back into half-sleep until Mum finally stirred and announced that it was time to get up. With groans and sighs they piled out of the cramped bed.

That moment in time, that warm, safe, happy morning when she knew, without even realising it, how much she was loved. It still brought a heaviness to Georgie's heart to remember the shock of how life had changed so quickly.

*Daddy*. She hadn't really talked openly about him in years but he was 'Daddy' and she felt like she was the centre of his world. It was only when, as an adult, she re-examined his actions that she realised, with sadness, just how flawed he was.

She remembered times of anxiety when her mum wondered where he was. He worked as a chef in a popular local restaurant. Fortunately for family life, once he was promoted to head chef he could leave the team to do the final clean-down and get home at a reasonable hour. But some nights he would be late, and sometimes on his day off he'd have to pop out to see a mate about something. Georgie knew that this sometimes led to tension or arguments but wasn't sure why: she only knew that when her parents said they needed a few moments to talk privately, she was not allowed to disturb them. They would go into the kitchen and close the door.

Sometimes she listened, but all she could hear were muffled words and an urgent tone in her mother's voice. There was never any shouting and they obviously wanted to ensure Georgie wouldn't hear, but she would still feel the gnawing grip of anxiety in her tummy. Eventually they would come out, and the worried look on her mother's face would quickly change into a smile when she realised Georgie was standing there, waiting for them. Her father would feign surprise to see her and would ruffle her hair before asking what was for tea. All back to normal, balance restored, or so it felt.

Years later, when Georgie was trying to piece the past together, she had asked her mother what had been going on then: what were they so worried about? Why all the hushed discussions? It was then that the pieces fell into place and she understood: her parents had a few money worries. They had fallen behind after her father lost his job at a local hotel when it had gone bust. Those six months out of work, with only a little money coming in from her mum's job, had put a strain on things. That was when her father got involved with a couple of guys who used to come to the restaurant. They always ordered the most expensive steaks and the best wine, and money didn't appear to be a worry for them. When they asked to compliment the chef, the three of them got chatting and had a drink together: so began a friendship. Georgie often wondered if they had targeted her father deliberately. Pretty soon they had learnt about his money troubles and offered him an easy solution, a few risks involved but well-paid so he would be mad not to do it just until the family cleared their debts. The restaurant provided the perfect meeting place for customers and suppliers, and her father was the perfect middle man – always at the restaurant and, more importantly, always *meant* to be there, so suspicions wouldn't be aroused.

Inevitably word got around and one night he supplied the right drugs to the wrong people. He was caught by undercover police and charged with possessing and supplying cocaine. The whole chain fell like dominoes; they had all been under surveillance for weeks. Her mother had blamed it all on her father's two 'friends', Robbie and Tony, for luring him into it. But that wasn't the way the police or the Crown Prosecution Service or the judge and jury saw it. Her father got five years. It was devastating but as ever, even in those dark days, he rolled with the punches. He assured them it was all a mistake but he would do his time and play the game so he should be out in a lot less than five years. Her mother cried, her father smiled and Georgie just looked from one to the other, wondering which face she was meant to put on.

And that's when the endless train journeys began, back and forth, to visit her father in prison. The visits always seemed a lot shorter than the time they spent on the train. And her mother was so tense on the way there and so tearful on the way back. She would never talk and was just constantly irritable and snappy. So she learnt to keep her own counsel, while the daydreams of the racing black horse and the wild and free Georgie kept her company.

Because she had so little experience of how cruel life could be, Georgie thought things could not get any worse. Even with her limited experience of life, she knew those endless years of prison visits would eventually pass and her father would be allowed home. Most of all she hung on to her father's promise that it would be 'less than five years, just watch'. But by the time she was eleven he had been in prison for two Christmases, two birthdays, two school years and there was still no sign of him coming home.

It was just after the second Christmas that her mother's howling cries, feral and uncontrolled, woke Georgie in the middle of the night. She hadn't heard the phone ring or the conversation, but it was her mother's frightening cries that drew her from a deep sleep to bolt upright. She froze for a moment, trying to work out what had woken her. Then she heard her mother's cries again and hurtled out of her bedroom. She searched her mother's room and the bathroom before realising the cries were coming from the hall. Her mother was slumped on the floor, her face in her hands with the phone lying by her side. Everything was a blur after that, a deliberate blur as the truth was too painful to recall in vivid detail. Her father had been taken ill, seriously ill. They had to come quickly to the hospital. It would cost a fortune because there were no trains at that time of night – they called a taxi and, in tight anxiety, fearful but hopeful, they sat hunched in the back. But it was all too late. He had died by the time they got there. The post-mortem revealed a brain aneurysm, undiagnosed and unstoppable. It had all been very quick and exceptionally cruel; he was only thirty-four.

Georgie flinched at the memories that were flooding back. Uninvited tears had started to sting her eyes so she turned away from the window to search in her bag for the newspaper she had bought that morning. She wanted to stop the memories, the sad path her wandering mind was taking her on. It was too painful and never got less so, no matter how many times she had revisited it.

As she pulled out the newspaper and smoothed the front page she heard the hissing of the brakes. The train had started to slow down. She checked her watch, they couldn't be coming into a station yet, could they? She jumped as a loud voice suddenly came over the tannoy speaker in the carriage.

**We apologise for the delay. A train ahead of us has broken down. We will keep you informed, but expect to continue our journey shortly.**

There was a collective tut and sigh from the other passengers in the carriage. Great, just when she thought she was making good time. She considered getting up to grab a coffee from the buffet car but a number of people had already started to file past her, stretching and yawning. They had obviously had the same idea and there would be a long queue. Georgie settled back into her seat and decided to give it ten minutes for the queue to die down. She picked up her phone and checked for messages before sending a text to her mum. Train slightly delayed, train in front broken down. They said we shouldn't be long, will keep you posted Gx

She hoped her mum wouldn't stress out. She did worry, and every time Georgie told her not to she got the same reply: "I've only got one child and she is very precious to me so I'm allowed to worry. I am your mother." It was always said half in jest and yet was loaded with meaning. Georgie would always sigh, roll her eyes and give the same answer: "Love you too Mum, always." And she always did, even when they had tested their relationship beyond endurance.

The stalled train and long queue for coffee forced Georgie to remain in her seat for a while longer. Seeing her reflection in the window sent her mind back to thoughts of her father's death.

The funeral had been a grim affair. There wasn't much money and no one in the family was willing to help with the expense, given the shame that her husband, a convicted drug dealer, had brought on them all. Mum's howled protestations that he wasn't a drug dealer but he had been set up, just resulted in more cynical remarks and ridicule from the family. The general message was that she was deluded and should stop kidding herself.

"He wasn't a druggie, he died of an aneurysm. It could have happened to any of you," her mother had shouted when she went to ask the family for help. But they had set out their position perfectly clearly, and there would be no good money sent after bad. "C'mon Georgie. We can manage by ourselves." Georgie's mother grabbed her by the hand and stormed out of the family home, vowing never to return. They never did, and Georgie felt even more confused about what to think and feel.

The day of the funeral was miserable, grey and raining. Georgie remembered people looking at her and Mum and whispering to each other, never taking their eyes off her. She didn't know what they were saying but didn't like the fact they were doing it, so she resolved to stay by her mother's side all day. They had gone to a local pub after the burial; a back room had been set aside for them. But the front bar was packed and the sound of the football commentary blasting from the TV and the roar of the drinkers every time a goal was scored made it a very uncomfortable setting for a wake. The event was quickly drawn to an end by her mother. She thanked everyone for coming and made their excuses to leave, saying that Georgie was tired. She didn't *feel* tired. She didn't feel anything other than lost, disconnected from the life that was now taking over from her previous happy cocoon.

The next few years weren't great. It wasn't until Georgie was seventeen and on her third counsellor that she could begin to articulate the reason for her unhappiness. She realised that there had been too many changes taking place in her life and that she had no control over any of them. She lost her father when she was eleven, just as she had just started senior school. At the same time, her mother had sold the 1980s new-build house that they could no longer afford and moved them into a one-bedroom flat above a dry cleaners.

Her mum had done her best at first. She made sure Georgie had the right school uniform, even if some of it was bought from the school's second-hand shop. And she applied for whatever help she could get to make ends meet. Her part-time job at the supermarket wasn't enough to keep them going. She could have worked extra hours, but that would always be the nightshift and there was no way she would leave her daughter.

So things were tight financially, although Georgie didn't

really mind and, in some ways, nor did her mother. They were too consumed by grief to care about holidays, treats or even essentials. Her mum was often in bed when she left for school and, if she wasn't working, she would sometimes still be in bed when Georgie got home. She would just lie there with the curtains closed, even on bright sunny days. Sometimes with Georgie's encouragement she would get up. Then she'd drag on an old dressing gown and sit on the sofa, staring at the TV but not really watching it. Georgie would make them dinner, beans on toast or tinned soup and sandwiches, and watch anxiously as her mother pushed the food around her plate. She was scared; she didn't know what exactly she was scared of but she knew she was scared, and it was to do with her mum.

Georgie also had other things to be scared of and other battles to fight. She could hide her mother from the sneering snobs at school but she couldn't hide their situation. She got free school meals, second-hand books and a bus pass. This led to snide remarks about scroungers and how someone looking like Georgie could afford to skip a few meals. She would suck in her tummy and turn her face away, pretending to ignore them so they couldn't see how ashamed she felt.

She had been so proud when she was thirteen and got her first job. It was only a paper round, but it helped bring some extra money into the home. And Georgie's little reward to herself was to buy a few sweets and crisps as a treat on the way to school. Eating was her one secret little pleasure, slowly letting the chocolate melt in her mouth or hearing the crunch of crisps in the rustling packet as her hand dived in. She knew she was getting fatter but, in the scheme of things, it wasn't her biggest worry. That was always her mother.

Just when she thought things couldn't get any worse, the girls in her class found out about her father. They were all sitting in the school canteen at lunch-time when Alison Spencer burst in and went up to the class gang, sitting together behind Georgie. "You will never believe what I just found out!" she announced in a loud gushing tone, eyes sparkling with mischief and malice.

Alison got the response she wanted as everyone stopped chatting and looked up at her. "What? What? C'mon tell us!" they all chipped in. Georgie turned round to see what the big announcement was and saw that Alison had her head lowered, whispering, and the others were grouped around her conspiratorially. Then the gasps and the exclamations – *No way! Really?* – started until she leant back and deliberately looked over at Georgie before feigning surprise. "Oh no! She's there. I didn't realise. Don't say anything." And every single one of them looked at Georgie then turned back into the gaggle and started giggling and sneering. Georgie didn't hear much of what they were saying apart from the three words *drugs, prison* and *dad*. Her heart sank.

That was the start of it. For the next three years Georgie went through hell, a slow, silent, endless, soul-destroying hell. They chipped away at her, day after day, bit by bit, until they made sure she knew she was nothing. When there was a birthday party, she was not invited but they all made sure she knew about it, the build-up, the big day and, afterwards, the post-party review. They wanted to make sure she knew what she had missed. If there were team games in PE she was the last to be picked, and there was always a collective groan from the team who had to have her. On school trips she always sat by herself. Even when she was one of the first on the coach, they would all file past her. She would sit quietly praying someone would sit with her just so she had someone to talk to, so she would fit in and look normal and not like the lonely loser. She hated sitting by herself, listening to the snide remarks. *Some people are so fat they need a double seat! Where's that smell coming from? Is it from Georgie Porgy who ate all the pies?*

27

It was Alison Spencer who started that name and it stuck all the way through school. Every day they called her that or sometimes Piggy Porgy. *Every* day. Then they would giggle and nudge each other and all the time watch for her reaction, feasting on her misery and delighting when they saw tears.

Even all these years later, Georgie felt a deep stab of pain when she remembered all that they had done to her. She could never remember saying anything or doing anything to Alison that could account for her sheer vindictiveness, yet it was always there. And she endured all of it in a stoic silence. She kept reminding herself that, because she had lost her father, nothing else could hurt her that much. Her form teacher had enough experience of girls to know what they were doing. When she had the energy she would rebuke them but usually she would tell Georgie *Just ignore them, they're being silly.*

*Silly.* It always amazed Georgie that the word used to describe their behaviour, their endless, low-level sadistic bullying, was that they were just being 'silly'. When her mum asked how school was, her standard answer was *boring*. Her mum said she was bored too, she hated the job in the supermarket with a vengeance; it was boring, monotonous and lonely. And somehow that gave Georgie a focus, something she could try to change and control. She couldn't change schools but her mum could change jobs. She kept encouraging her, taking the local newspaper home after her paper round to show her the *Jobs Vacant* section. Her mum looked at the adverts, but she wasn't keen. She said it didn't feel right, that she wouldn't fit in anywhere else. She said she was no good at anything anyway. But Georgie knew, somehow, that a change for her mother could improve things for both of them. She secretly came up with a plan and started to save some of her paper round money. Then she checked out all the hairdressers in the High Street, reading the price lists in their windows to work out which ones she could afford.

After weeks of persuasion her mother eventually agreed to

have her hair cut and styled. Georgie put her secret savings from her paper round into her mother's purse, walked her to the hairdressers that had seemed the most reasonable and gently pushed her mum towards the entrance, encouraging her to go in. *Go on. They did say you don't always need an appointment. Just try it.* An hour later her mother appeared, transformed. "You look beautiful, Mum," Georgie gasped, and for the first time in ages she saw her mum smile shyly. They celebrated with a coffee and a shared cake in a fancy café. Georgie saw her mother stealing glances at herself in shop windows as they walked home. As soon as they got through the front door her mother took time to admire her new look, turning her head left and right and smiling at her reflection in the chipped mirror in the bathroom. Georgie saw her chance. She got out the local newspaper again and this time they looked at the *Jobs Vacant* section together.

A month later her mum started a new job as an admin assistant in the local sixth-form college.

Georgie smiled as she remembered how proud her mum had been when she announced her new job, showing her daughter the letter the college's HR department had sent her. They celebrated with fish and chips that night and Georgie felt so relieved; something had finally changed for the better.

She couldn't do anything with her own life, but she had helped change her mum's and things would get better. They did, more so than even she could have anticipated, because the college was where her mum had met Tom. He was a lecturer who had been widowed two years earlier. He was still getting used to living alone with occasional visits from his two grown-up children.

Thinking of them both prompted Georgie to check the time. How much longer was this delay going to last? As if reading her mind, there was another announcement:

We regret to inform you that we will be unable to move on for up to an hour. Engineers are working as fast as possible to clear the other train from the line. Meanwhile, we ask for your patience. The buffet car is open.

Again there were tuts and sighs from the other passengers, but they were louder this time. Georgie texted her mum again to keep her updated before deciding that this time she *would* get a coffee. She asked the elderly couple opposite if they would keep an eye on her overnight bag, taking her handbag with her as she edged her way through the carriage.

As she stood in the buffet queue a well-dressed lady, looking tetchy and harassed, squeezed passed and asked a rather startled-looking woman if the seat opposite was free. Georgie heard snatches of their conversation. The lady obviously wasn't impressed with the parenting skills of the young mother she had been sitting opposite in the next carriage and had decided to move. Georgie smiled to herself. She recognised the expensive coat the lady was wearing and was in silent agreement with her; she wouldn't want kids' juice, sweets or sticky hands marking her coat either. James had bought Georgie an identical one last Christmas. She had worn it when they went to stay with Mum and Tom. Her mother had been very impressed: "Georgie! Gosh, look at you. How much did that cost? Oh Tom, look at her. Isn't she beautiful? What a gorgeous coat!" Tom had smiled affectionately at Georgie and winked conspiratorially at James as he handed him a beer.

Some of the passengers in the queue had started chatting with each other, speculating how much longer they might be delayed. Georgie ordered her coffee and, instead of returning to her seat, decided to stretch her legs a bit. She wandered to the end of the buffet car and entered the next carriage. There was only one woman with young children that she could see; she must be the one the well-dressed lady had been complaining about. The mother looked pretty harassed, trying to keep the toddler occupied and away from the baby who was drifting off to sleep. She lifted her head from the story book she was reading to the toddler to check on the baby, giving Georgie a clear look at her face.

There was something familiar about her. Georgie walked on, but more slowly as she kept turning it over in her mind. Something familiar and yet something changed. Where had she seen her before? Through work? Maybe at last year's annual conference? College? No, it wasn't work, that didn't feel right. It was the eyes that were familiar but they didn't match the hair; it should be darker, more wavy maybe? Georgie stopped dead still and a chill came over her as the realisation dawned.

It was her. She was plumper, with highlighted blonde straight hair rather than dark brown, but it was her. It was definitely her. There was something about the pretty blue eyes and the tight-lipped mouth that had clicked. It was Alison Spencer. It was eleven years since Georgie had last seen her and yet Alison Spencer could still make a shadow of fear creep up on her. She felt coffee splash on her shoe and looked at her hand; she realised she was trembling. She kept walking then paused in the corridor, shaking. Was it Alison? After all this time? Maybe she had imagined it because her mind had drifted back to those school days. She turned and walked back through the carriage. She needed to be absolutely sure. As she walked her eyes were fixed on the back- then side-profile of the woman, studying every detail. Yes it was her, it was definitely her. Georgie had heard her speak to the toddler and the clipped tones and nasal voice were unmistakable. She kept walking until she was out of sight then leant on a wall in the corridor, her hand clasped over her mouth to stop the shaking.

She caught sight of her reflection in the window opposite. A terrified-looking woman with wild eyes stared back. Her rage was as instant as her fear had been. Suddenly she was angry with herself and at how she had reacted. No! *No!* This was ridiculous. This was where it stopped. It was too much, not after all these years and after everything Georgie had achieved. She wasn't going to let Alison Spencer control her life any longer; she was a grown woman, not fifteen anymore. She had left those days and that frightened version of herself behind. This had to be brought to an end now. She stopped in the corridor beside the toilet and stood still, looking out of the window. *No!* she kept repeating over and over in her head. No! She would not let that girl have control over her any longer. She had left that awful school right after GCSEs. She'd been close to getting expelled anyway because of her truancy and disruptive behaviour. The school actually had the gall to suggest to her mother that she had *anger issues* and perhaps needed more professional help.

Her mother had discussed the *Georgie* problem with Tom, one of the friendly tutors at the sixth-form college. Her mother seemed to talk about Tom more and more. Georgie had met him a couple of times when he came to give her mother a lift to an evening event at the college. Once he took her mother to the theatre when he had a spare ticket because a friend had let him down. He seemed nice enough, but to involve him in Georgie's school life was an intrusion too far for her.

There had been an argument when her mother invited Tom back to the flat to advise Georgie about school. Initially, they misguidedly tried to persuade her to stay on after GCSEs. That was when they realised just how bad her anger issues were. Slammed doors, broken cupboards, smashed plates and foul language left her mother in tears and brought a watchful look to Tom's eyes. Each time the subject was broached, Georgie's reaction escalated. Tom seemed to understand that something was making her want to get away from the school, that something was seriously wrong. He gave her some much-needed cooling-off time and persuaded her mother that maybe she should be allowed to leave after all. She never did fully explain to them why she wanted to get out of school. It would have meant talking about the Alison Spencer gang, about what they said about Georgie and her mother. She couldn't bear that.

So, with Tom's intervention and support, she was given an out. He brokered a deal with Georgie and her mother which meant she could leave school as long as she agreed to continue her education. Tom wanted her to understand how much control she could have over her future. With his help, Georgie realised that her education was a way out of the pokey flat she and her mother lived in. She started studying for her 'A' levels at the sixth-form college where Tom and her mother worked.

She never once looked back after she left the school and her poisonous, vindictive tormentor, Alison Spencer. Away from the pressure of school and the everyday fear of bullying, Georgie began to flourish. And for once she really worked, almost obsessively studying books, paying attention in class and taking extra tests and practice papers.

This behaviour started to worry her mother almost more than the anger. Georgie seemed obsessed with study and didn't have any kind of social life. She never wanted to go out or see friends; did she even have friends? Her mother started to feel uneasy and she mentioned her concern to Tom over coffee in the staff room. He said he would keep an eye on Georgie and he did, ever so gently, with a light hand and a quiet manner.

Tom started to guide and encourage her. He took the time to get to know her, to identify her strengths and her ambitions and to help her pick the right subjects and the best classes for her. He suggested she join the college netball team as they always needed new players. Georgie declined; the feeling of being picked last for every team was still raw.

So Tom suggested to two of the players that they should persuade Georgie to join as a favour to him. And, because he was their favourite tutor and they had kind hearts, they got her to sign up. To their surprise, and her astonishment, she found she was actually quite a useful player. So her confidence grew, as did her social circle and her fitness. She joined some of the other players in their weekly gym classes and runs. Slowly, without realising what was happening, Georgie blossomed and relaxed as she started to shake off the shrouds of misery from her old school.

With Tom mentoring her and her mother supporting her, Georgie thrived. The day her university place was confirmed, they celebrated in style at a posh Italian restaurant in town. Tom insisted it was his treat. There was a gentle sensitivity and kindness in Tom's manner. He didn't try to be a father to her but he was the person she started to instinctively turn to for advice. Their respect and trust in each other grew. And while Georgie never commented and her mother never said anything, it was obvious that Tom was becoming more than just 'Mum's friend'. He was a frequent and welcome guest in their house and it gave Georgie the peace of mind she so desperately needed to know he was there for both of them.

A whole new world of possibilities opened up to Georgie when she started university. A different town gave her the chance to reinvent and re-establish herself, and she grabbed it with both hands. Her mother took the same opportunity and, during Georgie's first summer break from university, she was overcome with emotion when Tom asked her how she would feel if he and her mother were to get engaged. Georgie didn't say anything but Tom knew her answer when she hugged him tightly and he felt her warm, wet tears on his shirt. She didn't know when she was happier, the day mum and Tom got married and she cried, or the day she graduated with honours and her mum and Tom cried.

Georgie had gone on to a graduate programme at a city firm and she was now earning more, at twenty-seven, than Tom or her mother were earning in their fifties. And, best of all, the job had introduced her to James; funny, smart, loyal, tender James. He had thought her very reserved when they first met. In fact, he thought she was downright rude and aloof. It had taken him months of working alongside her, sometimes late into the evening, to establish a mutual respect. They'd had a few laughs and jokes along the way but nothing more. Initially she declined any offers of drinks after work unless a gang of people was going. She had definite rules and barriers that he couldn't quite work out. But his subtle enquiries among her friends and colleagues revealed that there was no competition; he set out with gentle persistence and good humour to win her over, and he did. He was the final piece in the armour she needed.

So why now was she standing in a train corridor terrified of some harassed woman with two children? Had all of it been for nothing?

Georgie realised, with shame, that she was practically hiding in the train corridor, shrinking away at the sounds of any footsteps coming towards her. It was pathetic. She looked out of the window, wrestling with her thoughts and trying to decide what to do next. Should she go forward or back? Maybe this should all be left in the past. Her phone buzzed in her bag; she fumbled to find it and saw a text from her mum. Hope all ok, journey not too stressful x Suddenly Georgie's face cleared and her expression settled into one of grim determination. She turned and walked back into the carriage, slowly approaching the woman. She swallowed and took a deep breath before she spoke to ensure her voice betrayed no fear.

"Hi Alison, how are you?"

The woman had been sending a text, making use of the short time the baby was asleep and the toddler was occupied with colouring pens and a book. She looked up, surprised to hear her name.

"Sorry. Do I know you?" She looked hesitantly at Georgie.

"Yes. Yes, you do know me Alison. We were at school together, remember? I'm Georgina Adams."

A flicker of recognition passed over Alison's face. She quickly controlled herself. "No. Sorry, I don't remember you." She gave a friendly, polite smile, trying to draw the encounter to a close. "Anyway, nice to see you. Sorry, but I have to sort something out. The train delay, you understand." And she returned to her texting with exaggerated focus.

Georgie hesitated. She had been dismissed. She almost turned to go but knew that would never bring her the closure she wanted. She resolved to stand her ground and follow through with her plan. She pushed some sweet wrappers and pens to one side and sat down on the seat opposite Alison, who stopped texting and looked up anxiously. "Look, I'm sorry but I really don't know you. Now will you please leave us alone?" she hissed.

"Really, Alison, I can't believe you've forgotten me. We spent five years together at the same school, St Dunstan's High. Don't you remember?" Georgie smiled at Alison, and held her gaze. Alison looked away quickly, starting to gather up some of the toys and debris around her.

"Gosh, St Dunstan's. That was a long time ago, and it was such a big school. I really can't remember everyone who went there." She put some of the rubbish into a bag and looked around for a bin. Seeing one at the end of the seats she moved to get up, but Georgie stayed put. Alison was forced to remain seated or leave this woman with her children.

"You see, Alison, I think you *do* know me. It's funny how you don't remember and I do. I remember it all very clearly. Maybe you don't remember me as Georgina Adams, Georgie. Does the name *Georgie Porgy* ring a bell? Or *Piggy Porgy?*"

At that, the little boy by Alison's feet looked up and laughed. "Piggy Porgy? That's a silly name!"

Georgie looked down at him and smiled. "Yes, it *is* a silly name isn't it? But it's a mean name too. It made me cry every time I heard it."

"Don't cry," the little boy said as he put his hand on Georgie's leg. He suddenly looked very serious. "Don't cry," he said again, and rubbed her knee.

Georgie put her hand on his and smiled. "Don't worry. I'm not crying, and you are very kind to worry about people's feelings." She turned and looked at Alison, who was staring at her with ill-disguised disgust.

"For God's sake, you never could take a joke could you . . . ? Get your hands off my child. Don't touch him. leave him alone. Yes, I remember you. More importantly I remember your family and what your dad did. Drug dealer, prison! How dare you speak to me? And don't you dare lay a land on my son. Have you no shame, coming up to me to have a little chat like we were old friends? Why would I ever want to have anything to do with the likes of you? *Now go away,*" Alison's voice rose from a hiss to a shout. People in nearby seats began to look around, mildly interested in any distraction that would break up the tedium.

Georgie's voice was calm and controlled. "Don't raise your voice, Alison. You'll scare your little boy. He was only being kind-hearted. I really do wonder where he learnt that from?" The question hung in the air and neither woman spoke. The little boy looked uncertainly from his mother's angry face to Georgie, who leant forward and ruffled his hair affectionately. Taking this as a sign that all was well, he turned back to his colouring book.

Georgie continued to stare at Alison and enjoyed watching her discomfort, seeing her trying to wriggle free from the situation. "You see, Alison, you obviously remember me and my time at school very well. I was a great source of entertainment to you and the whole class for years. You made my life hell and, even if you like to pretend you don't remember, I have never forgotten." She felt the breath catch in her throat, and consciously relaxed her tense shoulders. She was determined not to cry.

Alison looked flustered. "What's she saying, Mummy?" asked the little boy, suddenly regaining interest in the new friend Mummy was talking to.

"Nothing, honey. Keep colouring the picture. Grandma will love it." Alison scattered more colouring pens towards the child and leant over to Georgie. "Look, *please* just go away and leave us alone. I have nothing to say to you. I have enough on my plate to deal with and I am not in the mood to go over some ancient history from schooldays." She stopped; her voice was starting to falter, almost breaking.

Georgie examined her face closely. Was she faking something, just trying to get out of an awkward situation? "Don't worry. I'm not here to cause any trouble. I just wanted you to know something really, really important. Despite all the name calling, bitchy comments, isolation, segregation and bullying, despite all of that, Alison, I want you to know I am really happy. I am really, genuinely, truly happy. I have a great job, a wonderful boyfriend and great friends. My mother, despite all your efforts to backstab and belittle her, is very happy too. In fact she has re-married. He's a wonderful man who worships her for the kind-hearted, beautiful soul she is. I just wanted you to know all of that, Alison. Despite your concerted efforts to see how far you could push me, your attempts to break me, I am truly happy. You didn't succeed."

She drew breath. Her voice had started to tremble a bit before the end of her speech but she had managed to get all the words out without stumbling. She felt her face flush and her hands shake, but it was done now. She put her coffee cup down and got up to leave. Alison had been staring at her and now turned away to look out of the window, a creeping blush

38

colouring her cheeks. She put her hand up to her mouth and wiped away imaginary crumbs. Georgie knew there was nothing Alison could say, nothing that could change the pain of all those years. She smiled at the little boy once more to reassure him all was well, then reached for her handbag and rose to leave.

Alison spoke. "Georgie, look, I think you are making too much of it. We were all just kids having a laugh, just playground laughs. Really, you should learn to take a joke. Of course we all had our problems in those days. It's sad that you obviously couldn't deal with yours but it sounds like you have put it all behind you."

Georgie felt her reaction veer unsteadily between outrage and laughter. "My God, Alison, you really are a cheeky cow aren't you? Playground laughs? Is that what you call what you put me through? And what problems did you have with your big house and fancy holidays and gang of divas? And for some reason I actually thought you might had learned some new words, expanded your vocabulary a bit. Let's see . . . like for example *Sorry*. There's a new word for you, Alison. Sorry. That's not a word you understand so maybe you should practise! I am sure there are quite a few people who would like to hear you say it."

She started to pull away. She didn't want this; she wanted to leave matters as they stood after she had spoken and Alison had heard her words. She could feel her anger build up and she wanted to remain cool, calm and in control. That was how this was meant to end.

Alison looked away, brushing her hand gently over the soft downy head of her sleeping baby. She let out a long sigh as if the game was up, then started to speak.

"Please, Georgie. Look, yes, I *am* sorry. Maybe it did get a little out of hand. Wait! Just a minute, please. *Just a minute?* Sit down." Alison pulled Georgie's sleeve a little too desperately, knocking her off-balance. Putting a hand on the back of the seat to steady herself, Georgie sighed and, reluctantly, sat down again. She really didn't want to hear any justifications. This wasn't going the way she had wanted it to.

"I need to explain, Georgie." Alison held up her hand to stop Georgie speaking. "Please just let me explain. I'm not excusing anything, I just want to explain. We all had our problems at school. You weren't the only one. I had problems too. Mine wasn't exactly a happy home with an alcoholic father and a neurotic mother and . . . "

Georgie didn't give her the time to finish. "Seriously, Alison? You expect me to feel sorry for you now? An alcoholic father? *Really*?"

"Yes, *really*." Alison bristled and sat forward in her seat so her face was only inches from Georgie's. "The only reason he didn't lose his job was because he was the boss, though God knows he came close to the business going bust a few times. He was a functioning alcoholic for years. Drying out, then caving in again. And my mum . . . Look, I'm not getting into all of this but just remember that you may have had problems but you weren't the only one. The only difference between you and me was that I had a bit more money. Why do you think there were so many girls in my group who were happy to tag along? It was worth their while because of what they could get out of me. My parents were happy to throw money at me just to keep me out of their way.

"You see, Georgie, I don't think I was all that bad and to be honest you just liked playing the victim. Anyway, I needed something to divert their attention away from me. I was scared the girls in school would find out the truth about me, or hear about the police coming to the house, or that some of them would call unexpectedly and see my dad lying drunk and passed out on the sofa while my mum screamed her nut off at him.

"And you never really reacted to the jokes, apart from the

odd time when you went a bit mental and threw chairs around so . . . " Alison shrugged off the last few words.

Georgie stared at her. She was genuinely taken aback that all those acts of casual cruelty had been so easily shrugged off in a few words of self-pity. "For God's sake, Alison. I thought you were just a stupid bitchy girl but you've actually grown into a stupid bitchy woman. Can you really not understand, particularly now you have your own children, how cruel you were? You made my life hell for years . . . " She broke off as her voice started to shake.

Alison had looked away, her hand covering the side of her face. She looked back at Georgie. "Well, what about me and everything I went through? Have you not been listening? Why is it all about you? Haven't you heard anything I have just told you?" And the tears slowly began, coursing through the layers of makeup, dragging mascara like a murky watercolour down her face.

Georgie stared at Alison, open mouthed. "You know, you don't deserve those two sweet children and they certainly don't deserve you as a mother," she snapped. "How can you justify everything you did to me just like that? How would you feel if it was *your* child being ganged up against and tormented like that? Do you know I actually hesitated before coming to talk to you? I wasn't scared of *you* but I *was* scared of what you might say, because the only thing I wanted to hear you say was *Sorry*."

Alison looked at Georgie as she reached an arm around her son, protectively. "OK then. I'm sorry, OK? I'm sorry. But just remember you never once said anything back to me, you never retaliated, and you never attacked. You just seemed to absorb it. I knew it was getting to you but every time I saw you and your mum in town, walking arm in arm or laughing at a shared joke or her stroking some stray hair back from your face, I hated you. You and she looked so close, so loving and I . . . well, I suppose I was jealous of you, of that love and attention. You just irritated me."

To Georgie's surprise, she began to feel a creeping wave of repugnance for Alison who would never be able to understand or accept how cruel she had been. The nasty girl had grown up into selfish nasty woman. That galvanised Georgie. "Like I said, Alison. I just wanted you to know I am really happy. One day, maybe, you will be too, but you really do still sound like a spoilt, self-indulgent fifteen-year-old school girl. Do yourself a favour and grow up." And, with that, she got up and left.

Alison called after her. "Georgie, wait I haven't finished, please don't tell . . . " but Georgie had walked purposefully away and didn't look back. She stopped at the buffet car again, this time ordering a large glass of wine and some crisps. She took a deep drink from the glass and made her way back to her seat.

We apologise for the delay. The broken train has just been moved out of Huntingdon station. Due to the length of time we have been stationary, we will be making an unscheduled stop at Huntingdon. Any passengers wishing to alight there should prepare to do so.

Georgie barely heard the announcement; her mind was racing through her reactions, trying to decide how she now felt. She sipped her wine and calmed her breathing down.

This is Huntingdon. Will passengers leaving the train here please make sure they have all their baggage with them.

She looked out the window as several passengers got off the train with a mixture of world-weary and disgruntled expressions. The last to get off was Alison, clattering the pram awkwardly on to the platform and reaching back to help her toddler down. She hadn't mentioned getting off at the next stop, but Georgie hadn't asked her where she was going or where she had been. Alison punched a button on her mobile phone and pressed it to her ear. Georgie could hear her shouting directions into it. "No, I don't care. I've been on that bloody train long enough! Just come and collect me, now, from Huntingdon station. I mean it, *right now* . . . No, I'm not in a bad mood. No, I said right now, OK?"

She looked hot and snappy as she hooked various bags on to the pram and grabbed the little boy firmly by the arm. She glanced up at the train and, at that moment, Georgie caught her eye. She raised her wine glass in a silent toast, smiling at the tear-stained face, the crumpled clothes and the confused-looking toddler. Alison looked unsure, embarrassed, and lifted a hand in a half-wave but Georgie had already looked away as her phone bleeped with a text from her mother. Worried about you, what time you arriving? All ok? Love you lots. Mum x

Yes Mum, everything is absolutely fine. On my way. Love you too. Gx

# Time to let go
by Linda Cohen

MAX flew up the stairs of the underground two at a time. He dashed into King's Cross station, bought an expensive – but, to him, priceless – ticket, found the right platform and flung himself through the closing doors of the train. He had just caught it. Surely that had to be a good sign, didn't it? He was on his way.

He'd never been to York before. Of course they had talked about it, him meeting Emma's parents, but somehow they had never got around to it. She had always seemed reluctant to introduce them. He often wondered why, but thought maybe it was just a question of time. With no living parents himself, he would have welcomed Emma's into his life.

Max had been at Vision TV for about a month when he met Emma over the crisps at a mutual friend's leaving do. As a researcher, she had been shut away in one of the Portakabins outside and their paths had not crossed before. "Just imagine," she had said, later. "If Josi hadn't left the company we might never have met."

"Oh yes, we would," Max had replied. "You would have felt my animal magnetism penetrating the wall."

That had been eighteen months ago now, a whole year and a half of cinema trips, meals out, Sunday mornings spent in bed, sex, and more sex. "We are so good together," Emma sighed one night. "Nothing must change – I won't let it." Max smiled. He loved her naivety. Her delicate features, her air of cut glass vulnerability, fascinated him. He still could not believe that this boy from Leyton had managed to interest Emma, with her Home Counties accent developed at some posh boarding school. Such a contrast from his own upbringing! Fortunately nobody thought twice about his accent now, and he was just beginning to make it in the TV company which had taken him on as a runner. He'd even done a bit of editing on a series for Channel 4, where half the staff had come from a state school – like him – and some redbrick university afterwards. He fitted in perfectly here. *A kaleidoscope of social backgrounds*, he thought. *Just perfect.*

Max still surprised himself. Leyton hadn't been the ideal breeding ground for a romantic temperament, but he was discovering its shades and nuances with Emma. He started buying her flowers and surprising her with small treats just to see her face light up. Of course, at the end of the day, he never said no when she felt she had to give something back . . .

After one disastrous and exhausting day at work, having spent a weekday night together, Max and Emma decided that, no matter how urgent their desire, they would only see each other at the weekends. She sometimes brought an overnight bag to work on Friday, kissing Max goodbye on Sunday evenings. The arrangement worked for them, for their employers and certainly for Emma's flatmate, who felt able to take her boyfriend home while Emma was away. But mainly it worked because they seldom saw each other at work; they didn't feel the tug of love that goes with meeting the object of your affection in the corridor.

Max sighed as he settled into the train seat and looked at the other passengers. Everyone else looked so relaxed, so sure of who they were and what they were doing, so definite about where they were going, and here he was teetering on an emotional precipice – about to make the most momentous decision of his life. He had to get to York in time. He had to stop her.

He found himself staring at the young couple across the aisle and felt a twinge of envy. They had clearly just met, but he recognised the eye contact, open body language and shy smiles which heralded the start of something more. He remembered his and Emma's *before*, and a deep sadness overtook him.

Closing his eyes, he tried to sleep with the rhythm of the train but recent events replayed themselves in his mind. He remembered a few weeks earlier, how Emma had been sick soon after they woke up. She told him it was down to drinking too much red wine the night before. "Never again," she'd groaned as he held her hair back while she threw up. Then there was the weekend, about a month ago, when she had only spent the day with him after going to a hen do on the Friday night. She'd left him alone in bed after a light supper that Saturday evening, saying she had to get ready for an unusual Sunday shift on a new quiz show.

That last dreadful Saturday morning, after Emma had yet another bout of sickness, the penny finally dropped. "How long have you known? Why didn't you tell me? Why didn't you say anything?"

"About three months, but I didn't want anything to change between us. I wanted us to carry on just being us, with no complications. I just wanted it all to go away."

As her words stood between them Max stared, not recognising the Emma that now appeared before him. The carefree irresponsibility of his life evaporated in a moment. "How, Emma? How could you have been so bloody irresponsible? You're on the pill, for God's sake!"

Emma's frantic tears had merely stoked the furnace within him. "I'm sorry. It was Paris," she managed between sobs.

"I never thought . . . I forgot to bring the pills . . . I just wanted . . . her voice trailed away as she turned from him.

"You absolute idiot. Am I the only grown-up in this relationship? You played Russian roulette with our lives – and now look at us. If only you hadn't been so stupid."

That was two weeks ago now. He had let Emma pack a bag, without comment. Anger and hurt still simmered in his gut, and he merely glanced at her as she hesitated in the doorway before struggling down the stairs.

The next day, the flat had an air of abandoned emptiness. Emma's shirt was still on the washing rack, her perfume still beside his aftershave on the bathroom shelf. The fury that had driven him to throw their framed Parisian-holiday photograph into the grate had morphed into a dull ache of loneliness and desolation. But still he did nothing – he didn't know what to do, how to deal with this. He went to work in a sort of daze. He didn't see her. He heard someone mention that she was off sick, and still he hung in limbo.

What changed things was a chance remark by the production manager on the programme Emma had been researching. "Hey, Max, what happened with you two then? Emma's been off sick and now she's sent me her resignation. What's going on? She was a good researcher."

Max sat there for a moment before something clicked in his head. "I don't know. I don't know." The words spurted out of him, "I'm going to find her though. I'll bring her back – I've been a complete jerk, haven't I? Thanks." The last word was thrown back over his shoulder as he headed out of the door, leaving his colleagues looking after him in confusion.

Max left the office at a run. He'd think of an excuse later. What the hell was he doing? Emotions, plans, were playing havoc with his brain as he ran towards Camden Town tube station. So there was a baby. So he could handle it! What was important? Wasn't it the fact that he loved her? That she loved

49

him? Between them they would manage. He wanted a family, so what was wrong with sooner rather than later? Proposal, plans, began chasing across his imagination as he sat on the Northern Line, heading for Tooting and her shared flat.

They had never actually moved in together, so Emma had carried on paying rent for her room. His heart was hammering as he pounded on the flat's front door. Despite the urgency in his knock, it took a while for anyone to answer. As the door finally opened, he bowed his head in relief and said her name aloud. Looking up, he was surprised to see a stranger standing there, a woman in her twenties with a towel coiled around her head.

"What's the matter?" she eyed him suspiciously. "If you're looking for Emma Nicholls, she's gone. She moved out over a week ago and I've taken over her room. Actually I'm fed up getting all her post – do you have a forwarding address for her?"

Max found the woman's casual, near-hostile tone quite disconcerting, and stared at her. "Er – no, no," he replied. "I . . . do you . . . do you know where she might have gone?"

"Well, I asked around, because of the post thing, and I heard rumours that she had gone back to her parents in York. Sorry I can't help you any more than that." She was starting to look genuinely regretful, but turned away as a phone buzzed. "Oh – sorry again, got to go." And she closed the door.

Max leant his head against the familiar fading paint on the wooden door as his mind drained. How could she just go, leaving no message? How could she just ignore the last incredible eighteen months? "I love us," she used to say. How could she just leave? Surely she knew he'd get his head around it all eventually. Where in York did her parents live, anyway? Oh, for goodness sake – he'd come around here to her flat without even calling her. He had actually forgotten about his phone! He snatched it from his pocket and called, preparing himself to deliver the most abject apology. He got her voicemail and left a grovelling message. Then he texted – and for good measure he sent a Whatsapp. Facebook! Of course – he could leave her a private message there. He called up his *Friends* and scrolled frantically through the list. Where was her name? She wasn't there. SHE WASN'T THERE! What? She must have unfriended him. He was rooted to the spot for a moment, before adrenaline surged once more and his brain lurched into gear. Josi! Of course – her best friend, she would know where to find Emma. He searched his *People* file. No Josi. Hell, he'd deleted her number when she left the company.

OK . . . *THINK!* Max hailed a taxi and headed back to central London and Josi's new office, hoping she hadn't moved on again. The receptionist was checking her Twitter feed when he walked in. She hastily minimised, looking faintly irritated.

"Hello," she said. "Can I help you?"

"Um, yes. Is Josi Meadows here?"

"Oh. No, she's out of the office today. Do you want to leave a message?"

"No – yes – well, I just desperately need her help. I'd really like to speak to her, TODAY. Do you have her phone number?"

"I do, but the Data Protection Act means I can't give it to you," the girl said defensively. "You wouldn't like it if your number was given to every Tom, Dick or Harry who asked for it, would you?" Softening a bit she added, "I could take your number and ask her to ring you, if you're that desperate."

"Please. And could you tell her it's really urgent. I need to talk to her as soon as possible," said Max, scribbling his number on the scrap of paper that she offered him.

"OK." The girl turned away from him and reactivated her screen.

Max left the office, berating himself again for his behaviour. Yet he still couldn't quite believe that Emma would move away without a word, especially as she was carrying his baby. He stopped himself: HIS BABY. This was the first time he had actually put it into words. He found himself smiling at the thought, and was astonished at his change of heart. He had to find her, he told himself, to tell her how much he loved her and how they could make it work.

Max checked his phone every half an hour, but there was nothing from Emma and no call from Josi. Just when he was beginning to think it would never happen, the phone buzzed. Unknown number – Josi hadn't let him down.

"Hi Max! How are you?"

"Josi! Thank you so much for calling. Do you . . . I just wondered . . . " He didn't know how to ask. Then it call came out in a gush of emotion. "I've got to find Emma. I feel utterly desperate and I was hoping – praying – that you would know where she is."

"Max, I think I know what this is about," Josi replied. "But really I don't think it's any of my business, and I don't want to betray a confidence. I do know that Emma has gone, but if she wanted you to get in touch she would have let you know where she was."

"Josi, please listen. I know I overreacted and handled the situation very badly, but I was in shock. It's taken me far too long to get my head round it, but I really love Emma. I really do – and I'm pretty sure she feels – felt – the same. Please, *please* help me if you can . . . " There was silence at the other end. "Josi? Are you still there?"

"Yes I'm here Max . . . but I think you may be too late."

"What do you mean? Too late for what?"

"Max . . . Look it's not really my place to tell you this, but I think Emma has decided not to have the baby. It's probably best after the way you reacted anyway. She was so desperately upset, she felt let down by you. I think her mind is made up. She's gone to York to be with her family and get back on her feet. *A new start*, she told me."

Max shuddered. "What do you mean, decided not to have the baby?"

"Please don't make me spell it out, Max. You know what I mean."

Max's voice was strangled as he argued with Josi. "For pity's sake, just tell me where she is. I need to get to her." Fearing that she might take offence and hang up, his pleading voice softened in tone. "I know she'll regret this for the rest of her life. We both will! I have to stop her – and I love her. Please, Josi, I'm begging you, help me . . . " His pride was irrelevant now.

Josi sighed. "If I tell you, you have to swear not to tell her how you found out. But I really don't approve of what she is doing so, if you can stop her, I'm backing you. She's got an appointment – it's all arranged. She's checking into a clinic at eight tonight. Her parents are helping her. Don't think they're too happy though. She is going to stay with them afterwards."

"Addresses, Josi. I need addresses."

She told him the address of the clinic and Emma's parents' home address. Max hurriedly thanked her, then opened his web browser to look up the train times to York. If he ran he might just be able to catch the 15:08 from King's Cross. He had to get on that train.

With sweat pouring down his face as he ran along the platform, he made it with just a minute or so to spare. As the train pulled out Max fell into a seat, his heart thumping. Wiping away the sweat he prayed he would be in time. What would he say to her? That he had had a change of heart? That he didn't want to lose either her or the baby? All of that was true, but would she believe him? The ache in his heart was a physical agony for which the sole relief would be her forgiveness. His commitment phobia had dissipated. Parenthood had always seemed like a distant possibility, way down the line, but it would happen now – it *could* be happening now.

After a while, as he gradually calmed down, he bought

himself a coffee and sandwich from the buffet car and watched the changing scenery outside the window. He began to rehearse what he would say to Emma. Why didn't she get back to him? Why hadn't she rung? She must have heard the desperation in his voice? He had to speak to her, but it wasn't a conversation the whole carriage needed to hear. He could ring her from the toilet and tell her everything, pour out his whole heart, what a fool he had been, how he had panicked, how she and the baby were everything he needed and wanted, how she had to come back to him. Maybe this time she would pick up. Damn! Two of the toilets were out of use – typical – and the other two were both being used. He couldn't believe it.

As Max returned to his seat he felt the train gradually slowing down before coming to an abrupt half. *What the hell?* he thought. *What's going on?* The other passengers were muttering and looking around as the train showed no sign of starting again. He finished his coffee and sandwich, got up, looked out the window and paced up and down the aisle.

Several minutes passed without a word about what was happening. Other passengers became restless and started talking about the delay but Max ignored them all. He wasn't in the mood to talk to anyone – except Emma of course.

After a while, there was an announcement:

> **We regret to inform you that we will be unable to move on for up to an hour. Engineers are working as fast as possible to clear the other train from the line. Meanwhile, we ask for your patience. The buffet car is open.**

Max looked at his watch: nineteen minutes to four. Would he make it in time? He felt utterly helpless. He could do nothing but pace or sit, endlessly checking his silent phone, sending texts which remained unanswered, and learning Emma's voicemail message by heart. He didn't want another coffee and the smell of instant coffee in cardboard cups coming from the buffet car made him feel as if he was going to pass out.

Finally the train crawled into Huntingdon station and stopped, prolonging the delay even further. Max's frustration rose to fever pitch. He checked his watch for the umpteenth time: twenty to six. Would he make it?

He went over and over in his mind what he would say to Emma. Would she believe him? Did she even know how much he loved her? He felt a sense of desperation which he just couldn't shake off.

The journey seemed endless but he was first on the platform at York and headed for the taxi rank, telling the driver the address of the clinic before he had even closed the door. How far away could this clinic be? He wished the driver would go faster . . . He hoped he had enough cash for the fare . . .

Jumping out of the cab, and shoving the money into the driver's hand, he rushed towards the functional modern building and through automatic entrance doors which opened with a hiss as Max approached them. He elbowed a hesitant youth aside as he croaked Emma's name before adding "I *must* see her, *NOW!*"

The receptionist regarded him coldly. "Is she a patient?" Max nodded, gasping for breath, and she casually checked her screen. "In that case, I must inform you that no one is allowed to see patients once they have gone down for their operations." Her jobsworth reply showed her irritation with his tone.

"But she won't have gone down yet," pleaded Max, realising his mistake and trying to speak slowly and calmly. "She's booked in for eight o'clock. It's far too early."

The woman checked her list and sniffed. "We had a cancellation, so Ms Nicholls came in early. She went down to theatre at five o'clock instead."

"Are you telling me Emma has already had her procedure?"
Max couldn't bear to use the 'a' word. He felt stunned, shocked,
by the news.

"Yes. She was lucky. They called her yesterday and asked if
she would like to come in this afternoon instead of the evening.
It sometimes happens like that, people change their mind
about coming in . . . " Her words faded to silence when she saw
Max's stricken face.

He turned away from the desk so she would not see the
tears streaming down his face and sat in the nearest chair, his
head in his hands. Emma had done it – and she had done it
without him. It was too late to change her mind, too late to save
the baby, and definitely too late to save their relationship now.
Max knew he would never forgive himself, nor Emma, and this
was something he would have to live with forever.

"Can I see her?" He looked pleadingly at the receptionist
and she thawed a little, sensing his anguish.

"Well, she's still in recovery. Why don't you give it a while,
then I'll ring down and see if she's well enough to see you – if
she wants to. Sometimes a woman needs a bit of time afterwards
on her own just to get her head in order."

Max stared at her for a moment. When he spoke his voice
was low, radiating all the tension which was coursing through
his body. "For God's sake, just tell me where she is. I need to
see her."

"Don't take that tone of voice with me." The receptionist
resumed her former defensive hauteur. "If you continue to
address me like that, I'll have to call security."

Recognising the impasse, Max headed for the door to the
street. Somewhere, *somewhere* in this building was Emma. And
not just Emma, but a part of them both that they had destroyed.
He sat down on the nearest bench as a storm of unchecked
tears threatened to overwhelm him.

Half an hour later he felt a bit calmer and had regained

some control. Heading back through the doors, he saw there had been a shift change and a younger receptionist was sitting behind the desk. She looked up at him, appreciatively, and a hint of speculation crossed her face. Ignoring the flirtatious smile, Max looked beyond her. "I'd like to see Emma Nicholls."

"OK. Who shall I say is asking?" Her tone indicated that she had got the message.

"Just say a good friend," he replied, his tone filled with sadness. Then he added, "It's Max. Tell her it's Max, and tell her I really need to talk to her."

The girl spoke to someone on the phone, then nodded her head and looked at Max. "I'm afraid Emma is resting and doesn't want to see anybody at the moment," she said.

Max found himself choking up. "Look, *please* get back on the phone. Just tell her I have to see her. Please – it's really important."

The girl hesitated. She really didn't want to get caught up in this scenario. Indeed, it was one she had seen so many times. She always found other people's distress so awkward but, against her better judgement and still slightly influenced by a struggling glimmer of attraction, she tried again. But to no avail – Emma wasn't seeing anybody. There was nothing Max could do. He felt helpless in the situation.

Yet still he sat there, drinking the tepid coffee the girl had brought him in a forlorn attempt to make up for the obvious stress he was under. While Emma was on the other side of the door, he couldn't leave. There must be a way.

The exhaustion of emotion caught up with him and he dozed, briefly. He was startled awake when the entrance doors opened and a late middle-aged couple walked in. "Good evening," the man said to the receptionist, speaking to her in a clipped, formal tone. "We are Mr and Mrs Nicholls. We are here to collect our daughter, Emma." Max stiffened, and stared at them carefully. He noted their smart clothes, their air of authority. So *these* were the people she hadn't wanted him to meet.

Their faces were stern and the woman – Max had trouble seeing her as Emma's mother – was carrying a large expensive handbag draped over her forearm, her hands clasped in front of her body. Max wondered if she was using the handbag and arms as a barrier against what she probably thought of as *this frightful place*.

The receptionist glanced warily in Max's direction. She lowered her voice, but he could still hear her telling them the room number and giving them directions on how to find it. As they walked through the inner doors, he realised that he would soon have an opportunity to speak to Emma. He had to take it. His senses alert, he stared at the doors as if willing them to re-open. She would have to listen to him now, surely, after all they had meant to each other. Once she saw him there she would have to speak to him, realise that there had been some dreadful mistake. They could start again, there would be other babies.

And then he saw her. She walked through the doors with a parent at each side, holding her elbows and steadying her faltering footsteps. Her face was porcelain white, blue veins throbbing in her temples. He had never loved her more.

"Emma," he breathed.

She stopped. "Hello, Max," she replied, but her voice was as brittle as her expression. Max took a couple of steps towards her, but her father stepped between them.

"I don't know who you are, young man, but I think I can guess. Emma is not in a fit state to talk to you, or anybody, so if you could just step aside . . . "

"It's OK, Dad. I can do this."

"No, Emma. Look at you."

"Dad, just give me a few minutes. I'm fine. Please could you and Mum just wait outside in the car for a moment? I won't be long."

Her father was reluctant to leave Emma with this dishevelled young man whose agitation was palpable. Against his better judgement he ushered his wife through the glass door then turned to glare at Max, making sure he kept his daughter in view the whole time.

Max took his cue to approach Emma. He took her hand and cradled it gently in his palm. Her limp fingers were, like her face, pale and unresponsive. Words started to spill out of his mouth and he let his emotions carry him on the wave. "Emma, I am so sorry. I came to stop you as soon as I found out what you were planning. The train getting here was delayed for over an hour. I would have made it otherwise, please believe me. You didn't answer my calls, you didn't call me back. I love you so much, you must know that. I just want to be with you. I need to make it up to you somehow. Please understand . . . "

Emma looked at him, and he sensed her withdrawal. He saw the emptiness in her eyes as she looked at him, a coldness that was never there before. When she spoke her voice was ice-cold.

"You've had a wasted journey. There's nothing to say. You said it all two weeks ago, when you let your real feelings show – and now I'm being the mature one. We don't fit, Max. We never have.

"You see when I found out I was pregnant, I felt trapped, horrified. This wasn't the life I had planned for myself, not with someone like you. We are worlds apart, Max, even the little things, silly little things. You used to laugh because I only liked proper coffee and I used to laugh because you loved instant. I loved going to the theatre, but for you a good night out was the cinema and fish and chips afterwards. Oh it was fun at first. I let myself believe I could be happy with you, could live your type of life, but actually I was dying inside, crying out for someone more sophisticated, more in tune with the sort of life I wanted to lead. You've seen my parents. Can you imagine them having you round for Sunday lunch, welcoming you into their home? No, Max, it was never ever going to be forever."

Max stared at her, and now it all made sense. He had once heard her talking to her mother on the phone and her mother had obviously been questioning her about whether there was anyone 'interesting' in her life. He had been surprised when Emma said, "No Mum, there's no one. I'm much too busy working. I've got no time for men right now." They had been together a year when this conversation took place, and he remembered feeling hurt and surprised. In contrast, he had wanted to shout from the rooftops that they were a couple.

He remembered another call from an old friend of hers, Benedict, who was obviously inviting her to a party and suggesting she 'bring a friend'. "You don't know my friend," she had replied. "Not the sort at all to bring to a party in Wiltshire with all your jet-set friends. Best I keep him under cover here." And she had laughed her tinkling laugh, and Benedict had obviously laughed too. He was not invited to that party and the rejection left him feeling humiliated and upset. Now that he thought about it, there had been many times when she picked him up on words that he stumbled on, but he was so in love with her that he let it all wash over him and tried to forget the things that gave him an uneasy feeling.

Out of the corner of his eye, Max saw Emma's mother come in from outside. Ignoring him, she stood between the two of them, encircling her daughter with a protective arm. "Come on, darling. The car's outside. We're finished here."

Max's hand came up in an involuntary gesture of restraint, but Emma's mother brushed him aside without a glance. As she started to sweep her daughter through the glass doors, Emma paused. She turned back and spoke.

"I need to rest now. I need to get on with my life and you should get on with yours. Just go home, Max."

Refusing to acknowledge Emma's rejection, he called after her, "I'll phone you tomorrow."

He just caught her reply as the door of the Jaguar slammed

shut. "I blocked your number." Emma wound the window down, "Oh, and Max, just be grateful that the train was delayed for over an hour because, if you had got there in time, we would have spent our lives as two pieces of a jigsaw that never quite fit. We have both had a lucky escape."

With that the window closed and the car sped away.

Max stood in the dark, watching as the lights of the car disappeared from view. It had started to rain, just a little bit at first then great big raindrops. He was glad because now no one would be able to see his tears.

# I'll be there

by Debbie Hunter

CRAYONS, sweets and paper cups tumbled towards Viv as the train lurched forward. The older child let out a howl as his mother clutched her baby closer to her chest. Viv tried to sweep the onslaught of child-related detritus away from her and attempted to stem a flow of orange juice which threatened to dribble onto her boots, as the train shuddered to a standstill. God forbid that these boots get drenched. She'd paid a fortune for them. She squeezed her expensively clad feet further under the seat to shelter them from juvenile-inflicted damage. She had taken great pains to create just the right appearance before she left for this journey, planning to arrive elegant, attractive and enticing, not juice-splattered and dishevelled.

Viv watched as the young mother tried to reason with the toddler, promising him all manner of treats to stop him clambering over the train seat. She knew that the promises fell on deaf ears and wondered why the mother didn't know that too. Had Viv had children they would never have behaved so badly. Her non-existent off-spring would have done as they were told from a very early age, just as she had trained the young assistants who now worked for her. Had she had children . . . but she hadn't. *Too late for a family now*, she thought. She was still reeling from the shock of learning that Mandy would soon become a grandmother. She couldn't imagine her girlhood friend as a grandmother, still thought of her as a gawky, rebellious teenager. Yes, well past her time for happy families but not too late for a husband. This journey would prove that she could make amends for the past. Second chances did offer themselves and happily-ever-after could still happen.

God, those kids were whiney. How long would she have to sit here listening to them? Why didn't this train get a move on? She picked up the earphones lying loosely on her lap and closed her eyes, the welcome darkness blotting out her unwanted travelling companions. The warbling of a young Michael Jackson filled her mind with the past . . . *just call my name – I'll Be There.*

ʈɳɪʄʈɪɳɪʈɪʁ

She wasn't sure what hit her first, the blast of hot air or the blare of the music. It had seemed like a good idea when Mandy had suggested it. "Party at Cathy's – her mum and dad are away. Sure to be a crowd. Meet me there at 10." Mandy was right, there was certainly a crowd. Viv pushed herself forward into the smoky mob, apologising as she stepped on toes and knocked elbows. She'd never find her friend in this throng. She looked around the dim room trying to make out a familiar face.

"Hi! Fancy seeing you here – didn't know you were back in town." Viv turned to see a dark-haired girl, her shimmering catsuit catching the light of the glitter ball. Caroline Rowley – she hadn't seen her since they'd left school.

"You here on your own?" Caroline bellowed. Shouting in her ear, Viv told her that she'd planned to meet up with Mandy but doubted she'd ever find her now. "Come and join us – we're in the dining room. Grab a drink." Caroline indicated a row of bottles on a nearby shelf. Viv couldn't see what was in them but she picked one up hoping it contained something drinkable and followed Caroline, edging her way past entwined couples swaying to the music. The dining room was quieter, less crowded, and Viv followed Caroline as she made her way towards a group of people draped around the window-ledge.

"Everyone, this is Viv. You remember Isobel from school don't you, Viv . . . and Patsy? This is Nick, Patsy's boyfriend . . . and you know my brother, Derek . . . and this is Kevin." The last introduction was embellished with a giggle and a kiss. Caroline edged herself on to the window-ledge and cuddled up to Kevin.

Viv remembered the last time she'd seen Caroline, their final day at school, everyone declaring their lifelong friendship for each other, how they would never lose touch. She hadn't seen or heard from her since. Not that she'd been close to Caroline at school, thinking her bossy and spoilt. Perhaps the feeling was mutual, as Viv had never been included in her tight-knit clique. She was surprised now by her friendly manner but grateful for it. She'd be lost at this party otherwise. Perhaps Caroline had mellowed over the last couple of years or maybe she was just full of New Year spirit, eager to impress Kevin with her sociable manner.

"Hi everyone." Viv looked around the group. "Wow, Isobel! I'd never have recognised you – your hair is gorgeous, so different." Too late she realised she'd said the wrong thing. Isobel's unmanageable locks had been the butt of many jokes at school. Pointing out the change was probably not what Frizzy-Izzy, as she'd been known at school, wanted to hear, even though Viv had meant it as a compliment. She took a gulp of her drink to cover her embarrassment and realised it was neat vodka. She spluttered and caught sight of Derek looking at her, a half smile on his face. She hadn't seen Caroline's brother since her school days. Being eight years older than his sister, he hadn't been interested in her school friends. He'd changed for the better too, almost handsome. She looked away and started talking to Patsy. She'd wait half an hour and, if Mandy didn't turn up, she would go home. Not the way she'd intended celebrating the start of 1976 but it would be better than making small talk with semi-strangers, or worse still, standing alone at the edge of a darkened room, a lone wallflower trying to look as if she was enjoying herself.

Caroline and Kevin left the group to join the dancers and Derek edged nearer to her. She felt awkward and scrabbled around for something to say. "Haven't seen you for ages. What are you doing with yourself now?" she blurted out. What an awful question to ask. It was the sort of thing her father would say.

Derek's answer, "Accountancy," was the sort of answer which would have pleased him. "I've been articled to Booth & Bayne. They've got an office here in York now – and you?" Viv told him about the arts course she was doing at university and how much she loved it. He told her that he was very ignorant about arts, in fact couldn't tell his arts from his elbow, at least that's what she thought he said. It was hard to hear in this room. She tried to convey a smile at his feeble joke but she wasn't sure he saw it in the gloom.

She caught sight of Mandy and waved. Her friend just gave a slight nod, then turned her attention back to a gangly companion who was a stranger to Viv. Mandy picked up boyfriends like other girls picked up bargains. *Not much moral support from my so-called best friend tonight*, thought Viv. *Why am I not surprised?* She took another swig from the bottle and turned her attention back to Derek. She was getting used to the burning effect of the drink and, as it warmed its way down her throat, Derek became more interesting. She laughed at his humourless jokes and forgot all about Mandy.

The Jackson 5 sang out from the other room. "I love this," Derek said, suddenly becoming more animated. "Come and dance." He took the bottle from Viv, grabbed her arm and steered her into the room among the other dancers. She found herself gyrating to the music, the alcohol assisting in the pretence that she could dance. "*. . . just call my name – I'll Be There*," Derek crooned into her ear, wrapping his arms around her.

"Just as well you're studying accountancy . . . with a voice like that The Jackson 5 won't be needing you," Viv teased him. "Don't give up the day job." Derek looked at her with mock horror, and they both laughed. She liked his laugh and, although he was no pin-up, he wasn't bad-looking. Maybe this party would be fun after all and hopefully she'd have someone to kiss at midnight. She did.

They kept in touch when Viv went back to university. The friendship deepened when she finished her course and moved back home to York. She'd hoped to pursue a career in arts but this was proving difficult. Not finding a job she liked, she took a temporary position cataloguing exhibits at a museum. In the evenings Derek took her to the theatre, pop concerts and restaurants, always eager to impress her with the best seats in the theatre or the most expensive item on the menu.

He insisted on taking her to *The Golden Fleece*, his favourite 'drinking hole' as he called it. He was fascinated by its ghostly reputation, not a fascination which Viv shared. He laughed at her apprehension and tormented her further with gruesome details of the unfortunate characters said to haunt the inn.

She would have liked to have spent time with her friends but Derek got upset when she suggested it. "I've nothing in common with them," he said. "And their boyfriends seem so immature. Why do you need anyone else when you've got me?"

He showered her with gifts – Chanel perfume, slightly too sweet for her taste but Derek loved the idea of a Marilyn Monroe-scented girlfriend; chunky necklaces which hung heavily around her neck; Jackson 5 LPs. She was surprised by his love of Motown, at odds with other aspects of his personality. It wasn't her taste in music but she told herself that didn't matter. She loved having a boyfriend to take her out in the evenings, it made her tedious days bearable.

Viv wasn't the only one Derek aimed to impress. He turned his charm on her mother who, in return, fussed over him. His favourite food was always produced when he visited and her mother made a point of admiring his clothes and his hairstyle, or pointing out articles in the newspaper which she knew would interest him.

But his charms had no effect on Mandy, who had left York to enjoy the London lifestyle. On visits home she regaled Viv with descriptions of gigs, fantastic shopping experiences and, in her newly acquired 'London-speak', *far-out* restaurants. Viv wasn't sure what these were.

"I've got to find a new place to live, Viv," Mandy told her one weekend when she was back in York. "Can't stand sharing a bedsit with Patsy a moment longer. Why don't you come and join me in London and we can find a flat together?" she urged. "Tell you what, I'll send you a copy of London Girl. I've seen lots of jobs advertised in there that you'd love. Get out of York before Derek turns you into one of those fossils in your museum."

Viv had her doubts about life with Mandy as a flatmate but her remark about fossils hit home. There was only so much enthusiasm she could muster for the exhibits at the museum.

The conversation came back to Viv one evening after Derek had taken her to see *The Goodbye Girl*. The flatmate dilemma and Mandy's suggestion both played on her mind. "Do you think Mandy would be a more annoying flatmate than Richard Dreyfuss?" she asked as they got up to leave.

"Mandy would be annoying anywhere." There was no love lost between her and Derek. "Why?"

As they crossed the foyer and walked out of the cinema, Viv told him about Mandy's suggestion. He let go of her hand and turned to face her with an expression so intense that she thought he might be in pain.

"You're not seriously considering that are you Viv? Don't go." She watched as his anguished expression turned to desperation. To her embarrassment, Derek dropped to one knee in the middle of the pavement. Pain seared through her knuckles as he grasped her hand forcefully. Ignoring the amused looks of passers-by, he pleaded, "*Don't go*. Stay here and marry me." She looked at him in amazement. "I was going to ask you on your birthday – I can't let you go. Please say you'll marry me."

"Go on, love, do it!" A crowd of delighted film-goers had started to surround them.

"Get up, Derek. Everyone's looking." She pulled her hand from his grip.

"Not until you say *yes*. I will stay here on bended knee until you agree to become mine." The last two words were emphasised by a dramatic sweep of Derek's hand to his heart. Viv thought this might be more for the benefit of the rapidly increasing audience rather than for her.

"You know I'll always be there for you. Like Michael says, . . . *just call my name – I'll Be There*."

Derek . . . reliable, steady Derek . . . or wacky, irresponsible Mandy – which one did she want as a flatmate?

She looked down at Derek and wondered how long he really would stay there. She glanced around at the amused onlookers – Derek wasn't the only one waiting for her answer. She took a deep breath. "Get up, Derek – yes, I'll marry you. Now, please stop singing."

※※※※※※※

The knock on the door became more urgent. "C'mon love – we can't be late. You know what the vicar said. The car's waiting."

"Won't be long, Dad – just give me another minute." Viv looked at herself in the bathroom mirror. Who was this stranger looking back at her? She looked closer at the heavily made-up face and stared into the troubled eyes. *Be honest with yourself*, she reproached the anxious reflection. *Can you really go through with this?* She removed the pearl clip from her hair and took off the veil, then opened the door and faced her anxious father. "Sorry, Dad, I can't do it."

"Can't do what, love? Is it your veil?" Her father eyed her hair. "I can try to put it on if you like, but not like your mum would." He reached anxiously towards Viv's head. "No, Dad, it's not the veil . . . it's the wedding. I can't do it. I can't go through with the wedding."

Until then Viv had not given in to crying but the sight of her father's crestfallen face, full of concern, made the pent-up tears swell in her eyes. "Oh Kitten, don't cry." Viv felt the bodice of the wedding dress crushing as her father's arms encircled her. 'Kitten' only made the tears flow more. He hadn't called her that since she was a child. "It'll be alright love, we'll sort it out. Come and sit down." He ushered her into the bedroom and gently placed her on the edge of the bed, as if she were a porcelain doll, smoothing out the skirt of her dress as best he could. "It's just the jitters. Everyone has a bit of nerves on their wedding day. I bet Derek's standing in the church now with his knees knocking. Let me get you some water, or would you like something stronger?"

"No Dad – it's more than that. I've made such a mess of things. I should have stopped this ages ago, but I thought it would all work out. I thought I could go through with it but I can't . . . I really can't." Viv sobbed on her father's shoulder, mascara staining his crisp white shirt.

※※※※※※※

It was the conversation with Mandy the night before which had brought her bottled-up doubts to the surface. In the months leading up to the wedding Viv had drifted along with the excitement of it all. She'd felt smug as her friends 'oohed' and 'aahed' over the expensive ring Derek had given her, much bigger and more showy than she would have chosen. Any doubts she had about marrying Derek dissolved as she witnessed her mother's joy at the news of their engagement, the realisation that she would be the first among her circle of friends to be the mother of the bride. Viv found herself enjoying all the fuss of trying on wedding dresses and choosing the one her mother liked best, the one with the highest neckline and fullest skirt.

As soon as the engagement had been announced gifts came pouring in from friends and family far and wide. It was as if Viv was taking part in an elongated Christmas. Her mother and Derek fretted over guest lists and wedding cake designs in between discussions with florists and caterers. She felt strangely detached from it all, a bit part actor waiting for her cue. Caroline and Mandy were to be bridesmaids, but only after Viv overcame Derek's objection to her best friend walking behind her down the aisle. Watching Mandy try on her bridesmaid's attire the night before the wedding, Viv silently admitted to herself that perhaps he had a point. She looked ridiculous in the cerise puff-sleeved dress lovingly made by Viv's mother; Abba outfits were more her style.

"Honestly, Viv, what on earth are you going to do with this?" Mandy was examining the *Teasmade*, a gift from Derek's parents. "Don't they even trust you to make a cuppa?" She looked around the spare room at the collection of wedding gifts which Viv's mother had artfully displayed for the benefit and admiration of friends and neighbours.

"You're certainly going in for domesticity," Mandy said, inspecting the assortment of crockery, glassware and kitchen gadgets. She picked up an apron emblazoned with geometric shapes in orange and brown, the colour scheme Derek had chosen for their kitchen. Viv would have preferred a French-style kitchen in the blues and yellows of Provence and had felt hurt when he told her that it would look awful. "Get with it," he'd said. "For someone who has a degree in art you show an amazing lack of taste sometimes."

Mandy held the apron against her skinny frame. It looked absurd with the bridesmaid's dress. "I've got to admire you Viv. I don't think I'm ready for just one fella yet. I can't imagine spending the rest of my life with the same man. Bit like having ice-cream but only being allowed vanilla, never trying out any other flavours – don't think I could do it. Well, not yet anyway." She lay the apron down and picked up a champagne glass, twirling it in her hands to catch the light. "Are you really going to the Isle of Wight for your honeymoon?"

Viv had wanted to go to a Greek Island. She'd read about Mykonos in a magazine and thought it sounded so romantic. An island honeymoon, she'd told Derek when he asked where she wanted to go, somewhere we can walk hand-in-hand along the beach with waves lapping at our bare feet. She was mortified when he said he'd booked a hotel on the Isle of Wight. "Saving up for a house, Viv," he told her. "Can't do anything too exotic now."

Thoughts of vanilla ice cream had kept Viv awake during her last night as a single girl. Bland and one-dimensional, is that how she wanted her future to be? So different from Mandy's life in London where she was free to do whatever she wanted with whoever she liked.

She now sat alone on the edge of her bed, the discarded wedding dress crumpled on the floor. She knew she ought to hang it up – her mother had no chance of a refund if the dress was damaged – but she didn't have the energy. The strength in her body had dissolved along with her enthusiasm for marriage. Dressed in old jeans and a faded T shirt, she didn't care what she looked like. The enormity of what she had done, or rather what she had not done, was just beginning to sink in. From her bedroom window she could see her father in earnest conversation with the driver of the wedding car. The driver had removed his chauffeur cap and was scratching his head. Viv knew that her father was asking to be driven to the church to let Derek and her mother know what was happening. She could hear a small voice in her head reproaching her. *You should be doing that*, it told her. *You should be the one facing the music. It isn't fair on your father.* She turned from the window, trying to ignore her conscience and fighting an inner conflict of guilt and cowardice. By the time the small voice won, the car had left.

What would happen about the honeymoon booking? Derek would be furious that he wouldn't get the deposit back. Oh Lord, that wasn't the only thing he'd be furious about; she could hardly bear to think what would happen next. The small voice tortured her further, drawing visions in her mind of the beribboned car arriving at the church and her father alighting from it, alone. What had she done? She wanted to run away.

Her mother was the first to return, with Caroline and Mandy close on her heels. Various aunts and cousins followed, bringing an air of panic into the room. "Viv, what's wrong? Are you ill? Your father's gone with everyone to the reception – no point wasting the food, we'll have to pay for it anyway. Derek's in a terrible state. How could you? What were you thinking?"

Her bedroom was full of people, all talking to her at once. She didn't know who to reply to first with answers she simply didn't have. She felt like a pair of old-fashioned scales, a huge weight lifted from her on one side while a mass of guilt bore down on her from the other. Oh God, what had she done? Just as she was thinking now would be a good time to faint, Mandy came to her rescue. "Come on, Viv. Let's go outside. I think you need some space." She took Viv's arm and guided her from the room. "You've done the right thing. If you're not sure then you mustn't go through with it. It might have been better if you'd said something earlier . . . but it's your life and you mustn't waste it on the wrong man."

Viv stared at the computer screen. Technology was changing so rapidly and she knew that if she didn't keep up she'd be overtaken by kids fresh out of school. She thought she was the boss of her company but, in reality, technology was starting to make the rules. She resented giving way to technology; she'd managed her business without it so far, why should she give in now?

Her marketing people said that if her company didn't have a strong Facebook presence it would be left behind. She knew they were waiting for her input. She was aware of the business potential of Facebook, had even set up her own personal page although nothing much was happening on it. She would just have to get to grips with it. Maybe looking at other people's pages would give her some inspiration, although she doubted it.

Knowing she was wasting time, she clicked the *Friends* button on her Facebook page. Mandy's name was first on the list, and with one tap her life appeared before Viv; pictures of Mandy with her daughter, with her dog, on holiday with her husband, the rather bland Brian. Viv had never understood how madcap Mandy had ended up with boring Brian. Could only be a case of opposites attracting.

Soon Mandy's page would be full of the new grandchild. Viv found it hard to imagine her friend as a grandmother. She was surprised by the feeling of envy growing inside her. She'd never regretted not having children but now, in her fifties, she felt that something was missing. She'd had a few chances at marriage but always put the brakes on the situation before it could amount to anything. She'd preferred the role of business woman to that of wife. But this unfamiliar feeling of envy was gnawing at her. She would like to have a constant companion at this stage of her life; someone who really cared what she was doing, someone to talk to at any time of day or night, someone to just *be* with.

She was curious to see who else Mandy had befriended on

Facebook. She noticed the link to their old school and clicked on it. Black and white pictures of classes of girls, all uniformly clad, loomed up on her screen. Viv looked hard at them but didn't recognise anyone. The notices about the Old Girls' Association caught her eye. It seemed to be a very active organisation with numerous updates by somebody called Caroline Bennett and, intrigued, she clicked on the link to her Facebook page. When it appeared, she stared at the face smiling back at her; it was rounded, slightly lined, framed by blonde streaked hair interspersed with silver strands. A face she recognised, yet didn't know. Viv read that Caroline Bennett *née* Rowley was married, had attended Warwick University, was Chairman of the Old Girls' Association and had 200 Facebook friends.

Viv scrutinised the photo of Caroline. There was still something of the teenage girl in the expression – a whiff of superiority, hauteur almost.

Her fingers hovered over the link to Caroline's *Friends*. She clicked.

Scrolling down she recognised few of the names, even though they were probably former schoolmates. Halfway down the list she stopped. Did she dare? She clicked.

This time the face looking back at her was definitely recognisable. The likeness to Caroline was evident; age had painted similar touches but this was a face she would know anywhere. She looked into eyes she hadn't seen for over thirty years, and Derek's eyes looked back at her. Maturity suited him.

Before she realised what she was doing she had clicked 'Friend Request.' Frantically she looked for a cancel or recall button – too late. Oh well, she could always ignore him if he replied. He probably wouldn't anyway, not after what she'd done to him all those years ago.

But he did reply. A day later a message appeared. "Viv, is that really you? What a surprise."

And so began the correspondence, messages catching up on

over thirty years of separation. Initial guarded polite enquiries became more and more friendly. Viv gave him her email address and they began longer and more intimate exchanges. She told him about her interior design company, how she had been terrified to begin with and certain that it would fail. How her passion had made it grow and she now employed ten people in her tasteful premises in Notting Hill. How she loved living in London. How lonely a big city could be.

He told her that he was still living in York, that he was about to retire from Booth & Bayne, that his marriage had failed and that he had never stopped loving her. The last statement took her by surprise. She thought their correspondence over the weeks had been platonic, just two old friends catching up – this came out of the blue. She was flattered.

We apologise for the delay. A train ahead of us has broken down. We will keep you informed, but expect to continue our journey shortly.

Shortly. How long was 'shortly'? The baby was wide awake now and furiously demanding his mother's sole attention. The older child was trying to scramble on to his mother's knee, jealously pushing his sibling aside. Even Michael Jackson couldn't compete with that. She pulled the earphones out, reluctantly leaving the past behind. Derek had sent her the music after they'd made plans to meet. "For old times' sake," he'd said. "Did you know I learnt all the words of *I'll Be There* so that I could sing it to you at the reception? Bit ironic that you weren't there."

We regret to inform you that we will be unable to move on for up to an hour. Engineers are working as fast as possible to clear the other train from the line. Meanwhile, we ask for your patience. The buffet car is open.

An hour! She'd be *so* late meeting Derek. They'd agreed to meet at *The Golden Fleece* – his idea. *We can be haunted by ghosts and memories*, he'd said in one of his numerous emails. She sent him a text telling him about the delay. Almost immediately she received his reply. How annoying. Don't worry. I'll wait for you – I'll Be There:-)

She couldn't put up with these kids for another hour; she'd have to move. Reaching up to the rack, she took down her coat and overnight bag and walked along the carriage. She squeezed past other discontented travellers, some who'd left their seats in search of the buffet car and others who were just stretching their legs. The train was pretty full but Viv thought she could see some spare seats next to a woman gazing out of the window.

"Sorry – is it OK if I sit here? Can you hear those kids at the other end of the carriage? Couldn't stand it any longer! I know they're bored, but honestly . . . "

The woman looked up at her and gave a faint smile. Viv took that as assent and lifted her coat and bag on to the rack above the seat.

She smoothed down her trousers and settled into the seat, taking her phone out of her bag. She looked at the woman sitting opposite and cast an appraising eye over her in the way she would have surveyed a client's room in need of her design expertise. The woman could do with a make-over. With a decent haircut and the right cosmetics she could have been quite attractive. Viv mentally transformed her, imagining a classic hairstyle, elegant outfit and, looking in horror at the woman's feet, definitely new shoes. She was shocked to see the woman's bare feet in flip-flops, in this weather. Her feet must be freezing. Viv's toes, encased in warm boots, curled in sympathy. For some reason she felt compelled to speak to her, as if the woman needed more than just bodily warmth.

"This is a real pain, isn't it? I'm supposed to be meeting an old friend in York in a couple of hours. Goodness knows when we'll get there now. Are you going there too?"

"Oh, well, um . . . I haven't quite decided."

Viv was taken aback by this strange answer. Why would someone get on a train and not know their destination? "Oh, really? So did you just get on the train without having any idea where you were going, then?"

"It's a sort of day out. You know, an impulse thing."

An impulse thing? How odd, but then Viv supposed what *she* was doing was a sort of 'impulse thing.' She felt a peculiar need to reassure the woman, she wasn't sure why. "Oh, everyone should listen to their impulses from time to time. Opportunities rarely come round twice, do they?"

Viv knew she was really reassuring herself. She wasn't in the habit of getting on trains to meet up with an old love in the hope of rekindling a long-dead romance. You could put that down to impulse, she supposed. She wasn't in the habit of talking to strangers on trains either.

The woman didn't reply, making Viv feel awkward. She felt impelled to keep talking to her if only to stop the woman dissolving in to tears, which Viv sensed she was about to do. She listened to herself gabbling words which tumbled out of her mouth before the sentences were properly formed in her brain.

"Well, you should go to York now you've got this far. The Minster is something else. I love those old buildings – they all seem so permanent. You know – we live in a world where nothing stays the same for five minutes and they've been there for a thousand years! They're so – secure, aren't they?"

"Is anything ever permanent or secure?" The woman's words were bitter as tears formed in her eyes.

"Of course – hey, are you OK?" Now Viv was really worried. The woman looked as if she was about to have a breakdown. Viv leant across to her and put her hand on to her arm, hoping to convey sympathy and concern.

"Whatever's the matter? Are you feeling alright?"

"No, I'm not 'alright' actually." The voice was so low Viv had to bend forward. "I'm running away."

The defiance in the woman's tone alarmed Viv. "Really? What from?"

"My husband – my home – my life."

As if floodgates had opened, the woman poured out her heart and Viv couldn't believe what she was hearing. She listened while the woman told her why she was escaping, why she looked the way she did, why she needed someone to confide in. The words flowed from her as if she had kept them pent up for months. Viv was appalled by what she heard. And all the time the woman was speaking she kept looking around as if expecting to see someone behind her, an eavesdropper listening to her tearful confession.

"So now you know it all, all about my wasted life, my bastard of a husband . . . and why I'm running away. And I don't even know your name."

Viv knew about abused women, of course she did. She knew that they came from all backgrounds; rich, poor, educated, ignorant. To the best of her knowledge she had never met a victim before. She was surprised how much this woman's story affected her, how it shocked her to the core. The feeling was almost physical, as if a stranger had dug her in the ribs. How lucky she was never to have been in that situation. She felt an overwhelming gratitude for her life of independence, solitary though it may have been at times.

"It's Viv – my name is Viv." Was this chance encounter a sign, a warning that she was about to repeat a terrible mistake? The woman had jolted her out of her silly romantic daydream and brought her face-to-face with reality. She took a long look at the person who would never know she had been a saviour. She had to help her.

Viv's phone buzzed making the woman jump. A text from

Derek: I'm at The Golden Fleece waiting for you. Now and for ever – I'll be there.

She thought how strange it was that, at the start of this journey, these words would have delighted her. Now they filled her with dread and unease.

She saw the woman watching her. The expression on her face reminded Viv of a trapped animal released into the wild and panicking at its freedom, not knowing in which direction to run.

Viv hesitated for a split second then tapped in her reply: Sorry – I won't be there.

# Run rabbit run

by Angela Haward

L AURA is gazing at the passing fields when the train lurches to a halt. Bags stored on racks jostle uncomfortably and people glance up momentarily from their phones and iPads. She clutches her bag closer and shrinks back into her seat. Deep in the pit of her stomach, a murmur of apprehension stirs. *Don't be ridiculous. He couldn't have.* She glances round the carriage, seeking reassurance. *Stop it. This is just a short delay – points or something. It'll be fine.*

But with each passing minute, her unease mounts. Finally, the speakers click and crackle throatily.

We apologise for the delay. A train ahead of us has broken down. We will keep you informed, but expect to continue our journey shortly.

Laura's restless fingers click the clasp of her bag. *How much longer?* Ten more minutes creak by before the tannoy sputters again.

We regret to inform you that we will be unable to move on for up to an hour. Engineers are working as fast as possible to clear the other train from the line. Meanwhile, we ask for your patience. The buffet car is open.

A whole hour! *We've only just left Stevenage – it's too close.* Laura feels her fragile courage shattering as her fellow passengers shift restlessly in their seats. Mobile phones are deployed and irritated murmurs rise all round her.

Laura feels a draught round her feet. She'd only stopped to pick up a pair of flip-flops in her headlong rush for King's Cross. No time to be trying on footwear. The March day is cool and she misses her coat. At least he left that handbag in the room so she has a brush. She is conscious that her hair is badly in need of a wash.

"Sorry – is it OK if I sit here? Can you hear those kids at the other end of the carriage? Couldn't stand it any longer! I know they're bored, but honestly . . . "

Laura looks up at a woman of about fifty, her lacquered coiffure anchored in its expensive bob, her tailored trousers and coat oozing designer chic. Why would she want to sit by me? She smiles wanly as the woman rustles into the seat.

"This is a real pain, isn't it? I'm supposed to be meeting an old friend in York in a couple of hours. Goodness knows when we'll get there now. Are you going there too?"

Laura hesitates. Mistrust has become a way of life.

"Oh, well, um . . . I haven't quite decided."

She realises instantly that this is the wrong answer – it just begs further questioning and the woman doesn't disappoint, her curiosity clearly piqued.

"Oh, really? So did you just get on the train without having any idea where you were going, then?"

Laura feels her heart pounding as her brain whirs round possible replies.

"It's a sort of day out, You know, an impulse thing."

"Oh, everyone should listen to their impulses from time to time. Opportunities rarely come round twice, do they?"

Laura has the feeling that the woman is referring to something in her own life but thinks better of questioning her about it.

"Well, you should go to York now you've got this far. The Minster is something else." The woman obviously feels like chatting. "I love those old buildings – they all seem so permanent. You know – we live in a world where nothing stays the same for five minutes and they've been there for a thousand years! They're so – secure, aren't they?"

"Is anything ever permanent or secure?" The words are out before Laura can pass them through her mental sieve. She hears the bitterness in her tone and is embarrassed to feel a tear forming.

"Of course – hey, are you OK?" The look of genuine concern on the stranger's face lights a fuse in Laura's mind. She can feel the imminence of the explosion. The desolation of her situation washes over her and the desire to share her fear is overwhelming. The woman leans across the gap between them and lays a hand on Laura's clenched fists. "Whatever's the matter? Are you feeling alright?"

*Should I tell her? Is that giving too much away? Oh, what the hell? I'll never see this woman again.* "No – I'm not alright, actually." Her voice is almost inaudible, but she glances up at the woman and sees only empathy. She's been so alone in the burnt out shell of her past.

There is a challenge in her voice as she says, "I'm running away."

The drama of the statement produces the expected reaction. "Really? What from?"

With the briefest of hesitation, Laura looks directly at her companion for the first time.

"My husband – my home – my life."

\*\*\*

I love him. I know I do. No one ever wanted to know every detail of my life before. No one has ever been that interested. They certainly didn't want to know at school anyhow. Suzy Smithson made sure of that. I was *Loopy*

*Laura* or *The Runt* when she felt particularly vicious. And the others loved it. They used to lay in wait near the top of my road and giggle about me to each other as I walked past, head down, not looking. Then one would shout, *Hey, Skullface . . .* or *Mind the drain, Stick Insect – your mates are waiting for you at the bottom.*

I never told Mum. She was just as bad really. I can still hear her. "For God's sake, Laura, get over yourself. You're so bloody miserable – you look just like your father, and I don't want to think about him every time you walk through the door. And get rid of those trousers. You look like a Belsen victim. Oh, just go upstairs. I can't bear to look at you."

But Peter strokes my face and tells me I'm beautiful, he loves my 'dark, brooding eyes', my 'porcelain skin'. I'm his Princess . . . think of that! I love it! I love how he holds me, how he draws me to him like he could crush me. He makes me feel so safe, protected somehow. And when a man comes towards us, he puts his arm round my shoulders and glares at the bloke. As if anyone else would fancy me, anyway! He says I belong to him.

*\*\*\**

I never imagined myself in a place of my own – but I'm in it. I'm just sitting on Our Sofa. It deserves capital letters. We got it yesterday from the second-hand furniture store in Willesden – the Harrods of the High Street, apparently. I'm in Our Lounge. Upstairs, there's The Bathroom, Our Bedroom, a Spare Bedroom – for my friend Jenny, maybe – and the Box Room. Yes, there's a box room – just big enough for a cot. I close my eyes for a moment. I can see the little quilt I'm going to buy from that stall in the market. I can hear the musical mobile tinkling. A huge bubble rises inside me . . .

"Peter – let's have a baby!" It's out.

"What? What did you say?"

"A baby! It's been two years – I know we never really talked about it, but we've got the house now and there's the perfect room upstairs and . . . "

"No!"

I stop in mid flow. "Is that all you can say – no?" I feel chilled with shock at the vehemence of his reaction. A tiny worm of fear begins to writhe somewhere in my stomach.

"Yes, it's all I can say. We never discussed it because we didn't need to. We don't need another person in this family. We are the family. We are enough. You are enough for me and I am enough for you. End of story." His eyes are glittering with an expression I have been able to ignore until now.

He gets to his feet and – I feel threatened. The worm has become a snake, uncoiling inside me.

"This has got to be that bloody Jenny. Interfering cow."

A searing anger overrides my apprehension. Jenny's the first real friend I've managed to make and hang on to. Before I met Peter, we used to go out on a Friday after work. I don't do that now – but she still phones every week. I need her. Yes, I did talk to her about babies – she's having one after all and – I'm shouting now.

"Jenny hasn't done anything at all – I just thought . . . "

The phone adds its jangling voice to the row. Oh the timing – it's Wednesday. Of course, it'll be her.

"Speak of the devil . . . "

He's too quick for me and snatches up the receiver. "What do you want?"

I hold out my hand for the phone. I can feel my cheeks flaming and I try to stare him out. He stares back with intimidating directness and moves to stand right in front of me, bristling with pent-up aggression. But his voice is barren.

88

"No – she's out. Sorry about that, Jenny. And she's out next Wednesday and the one after that. In fact it's a sad fact that she'll always be out when you call. So don't bother."

He slams down the receiver, and I burst. I am rushing up to our bedroom. And I can hear his measured footsteps coming up the stairs behind me.

\*\*\*

We're walking to work. He's beside me, holding my hand. It's sweaty and repulsive. He's been coming with me for two weeks now. He used to leave home early and I'd follow on. But since I mentioned the baby, since he scared Jenny off, he's made me go in at seven-thirty with him. Maybe, if I go along with it all, he'll change his mind about the baby – maybe . . . We don't talk. When a man walks past, he just watches my face. I look at the ground.

I can't tell them at work, can I? They'd never believe me. He's *Jolly Peter*, the ideal boss, the good bloke. He cracks jokes, flirts with all the women, joshes the men, makes the money – and me? I'm just another secretary. I know they all ask themselves what on earth he sees in me. I feel like *The Runt* again.

He'll be there tonight too. Waiting in the lobby at five-thirty, chatting to Anna on reception like he's the most affable chap in the world. And Anna will look at me with eyes that remind me of my mother.

Then we'll go home and he'll watch me get the dinner. It's fish tonight, with potato and broccoli. He'll just sit there, like he's been doing for months. Watching me. Maybe he's going mad – or I am. And he won't talk any more. He says he can't think if we talk and he needs to think. Why does he need to think? What does he think about? I don't know.

\*\*\*

I'm crying. The fish and potato are in the bin and all the broccoli is piled on my plate. It's overcooked – soggy as a wet sock and about as tasty. He's watching me force it into my mouth. I just forgot, I told him. I was busy turning the fish and mashing the potato and I forgot the broccoli. I'm sorry, OK? He's going to send out for a pizza – after he's watched me gagging on the broccoli. He's smiling – and it's like watching ice crack.

***

I'm in the shower. The water is freezing, he made sure of that. It's the rest of my punishment. He is standing in the doorway, watching me as I try to wash, naked, shivering, beyond humiliation. I know what will happen after the shower. It happens every night now, sometimes twice, sometimes three times. I know it's a power thing. But I am without power, a dead battery. He watches me shower as a sort of prelude, an overture to his sexual symphony. Only to me it's a cacophony – a discordant clash of bodies when one is a tuba and the other a piccolo. But maybe this time . . . ?

***

I'm curled up on the sofa. I'm not dressed. My eyes are burning and swollen and my whole body is trembling like it will fall apart. I'm not going to work anymore – not tomorrow, not ever. He told our colleagues I'm going to visit family in Australia, there's been an emergency. I have no family – not there and not here. I don't even know where Mum lives now. He has no family either, since his dad died of that stroke donkey's years ago. So now everyone at the office thinks he got me a last minute plane ticket and it would be better if they replaced me as I'm thinking of a career change when I get back. I no longer have the energy to fight him. I have nowhere to go. I have no money. Useless.

90

So I'm listening as he turns the key in the front door and walks to his car. The blinds are down. The windows are closed. It's stifling. I look at the CCTV camera in the corner. I know he'll be checking it on his phone as he drives to Cockfosters, to the office I've never seen, nor ever likely to. He'll be checking them all – even the bathroom. I can't even have a pee without thinking he might be watching me. And all the time he'll be playing hale-fellow-well-met with my former colleagues for all the world as if he is normal, as if I am normal, as if we are happy.

***

"What are you doing?"

He is ignoring me – again. He only answers when he chooses, not when I want him to.

I can see what he's doing. I don't need to ask again. The drill shrieks through the house as he hollows out locks on every door and window. He's bought a job lot of brass door handles with locks and keys and he's fitting them. I know why. Oh God, I know why.

***

This is why. I've been here for eight hours. Eight hours since the new key grated in the lock. Eight hours since I heard his footsteps retreating down the stairs and the front door close. This is the longest yet. Usually he is in the house and he takes me to the toilet every couple of hours. This time he has left me his grandmother's antique chamber pot – and I have had to use it. There's a bottle of water in here – and a bunch of bananas. Thoughtful. I hate bananas.

This time, I looked out of the window while he was at work, you see. I took a risk – I was desperate to see someone other than him. I tried to make it so it didn't look like I was looking. There was a chink at the side of the

91

blind and I positioned myself on the sofa with my back to the camera – and I could just make out the children walking to school, Marcus, in the house opposite, mowing his lawn. But in my husband's crazy head, I was flaunting myself to attract attention, prostituting my charms to the locals.

This is the box room. It's six foot by eight, with a small window. There is an unmade single bed against the wall, an empty cupboard in the corner and the shoddy boxing round the soil pipe running beneath the window, built by the son of Heath Robinson and with gaps a mouse could crawl through. The nursery of my withered dreams has become my prison.

\*\*\*

I'm looking at his wallet – his big, fat, overstuffed wallet. I know he gets £250 out every four days – he told me. God knows how he gets through it. He's been taking me to the supermarket for months now. We spend about £50 a week on food, always from the reduced section. Then he expects me to make out-of-date groceries last the whole week and still be palatable. As for the rest – maybe he's a compulsive gambler. Maybe he spends it all on prostitutes – but hey, he gets that for free. I don't care.

The wallet is looking right back at me. It almost speaks to me. He's in the bathroom. He took the paper, so I know he'll be a while. I can do this. I can. Without further hesitation, I extract a £10 note. It is old and crumpled and someone has spilt something unmentionable on it, but it represents a hint of freedom. He won't count it – will he? No – he thinks he has crushed any initiative I might once have had. It wouldn't occur to him that I'd be capable of robbing him.

I hear water running upstairs. I thrust the money up my sleeve and push a hanky after it to hold it in. It shouldn't be difficult to engineer a misdemeanour which will see me back in the spare room later. I know exactly where I can hide it.

\*\*\*

"I bought you this."

"What?" I look up listlessly from the sofa.

"Show a bit of interest, for God's sake! It's a phone. I thought you'd like it."

I am utterly speechless. He never buys me anything anymore. The days of flowers, chocolates and fluffy animals are long gone.

"Why? Who would I ever speak to now?"

"Me, you ungrateful cow. Your husband."

"We've got a land line."

"Yes, but sometimes you're in the spare room, aren't you? You can't reach the land line. I can call you if I'm – worried."

"You never talk to me at all when you make me go in there . . . "

"But I might want to."

I look at the phone in his hand. It's ancient – one of those tiny Nokias that were around ten years ago, the last time I had my own mobile.

"It's no good checking – there aren't any numbers in it – except mine. That'll be all you need. And I'll hang on to it for now."

I say nothing. There's nothing to say. My mind is empty.

\*\*\*

It's been three days this time. Three whole bloody days. I am exhausted. This time I broke all his rules and he is making me pay. I spoke to a man. Well, to be truthful, the man spoke to me. It was Marcus, the bloke over the road. He looks like a *Marcus*. Tall, thirty something, a bit Ross Poldark-ish (I used to love Winston Graham). He sounds like one too – public school, you know. Anyway, Marcus came to the door. He wanted to ask if we had an electric drill he could borrow – he'd heard it when Peter installed the locks. I'm not supposed to go to the door but Peter was in the garden, doing something in the shed. The outside doors aren't locked when he's in. I felt a flicker of something in my head, like a small flame igniting amongst ashes long extinguished . . . and I answered the door. Marcus looked nonplussed at first.

"Oh, I haven't seen you for ages. I wasn't sure you and Peter were still together."

"Yes, we're still here." I thought about saying something. But how could I get him to understand in the couple of minutes I might have.

Anyway, he launched into some spiel about why he needed the drill. I wanted him to go, but I couldn't think how to get rid of him without being utterly rude – and there was still a tiny part of me that didn't want him to go at all. He was the first person, other than my tormentor, with whom I had had any contact for – oh, God knows how long. The inevitable happened. Peter appeared without warning around the side of the house. I hadn't heard him coming. Marcus had one foot in the door, expecting to be asked to wait inside.

"Go back indoors, Laura. I'll handle this," was all he said to me. But I saw his eyes. I melted back into the darkness of the house.

And now I am here, frustrated, frightened – but for the first time in years, clutching at a glimmer of hope. The flame has caught.

I remember the hostages in Lebanon in the eighties – Terry Waite, John McCarthy and the Irish one – I could never remember his name. They must have felt like this. They used to escape into their own fantasy worlds to pass the time. But I have dared to banish fantasy. Because I have been making a plan.

No one is going to help me, you see. They have forgotten me. I have finally understood that I have to do something or I shall die here and I will only have one mourner. I am leaving.

There are problems, of course – ones I couldn't work out. Like I haven't washed for three days. He has taken me to the toilet, but that's all. He hasn't spoken – but each time the key grates in the lock, my courage flows instead of ebbing away. Also, I am only wearing slippers, which stand out a bit on the street. Maybe they will take me for a bag lady who has lost her bag. I almost make myself laugh now. Except I have got a bag. He threw it in the room after me when he marched me in. It's an old one of his mother's – circa 1965, faux leather with a clasp top. There's nothing in it except a hairbrush, an emery board, a packet of tissues – and the phone he 'gave' me a couple of days ago. There was no explanation – he just stared at me before he closed the door and, for some warped reason I cannot begin to imagine, his lips stretched into a sort of smile.

So this is the plan. It's time. My heart is pounding and my throat is squeezed tight. I am panting as if I've just run a marathon. First of all – tissues. They're all I've got. I'm stuffing them in the camera lens. I reckon I've got fifteen minutes at the most before he notices, maybe less. I don't know how often he checks his computer at work.

Now – the money. I can get eight fingers in the gap at the top of the panelling and I'm wrenching at it with all my strength. A fingernail rips and I feel splinters embed themselves in my palms. Finally, it gives. Rusty nails are prised away from crumbling wood and I fall backwards as it is suddenly released. The cash is scattered along the boxing amongst mouse droppings. They have clearly tried nibbling it but maybe the toxic ink put them off for the notes are mostly intact. I haven't time to count it, but there are at least twenty notes, if not more. I stuff them into the bag and with barely a pause, I tackle the window. I expect it to be locked and am prepared to smash it, but Providence must be on my side today. The lock is hanging from the frame. I'm sure it was screwed shut yesterday – I noticed it as he let me out to the bathroom, while he waited in my prison, casually tossing the key in his hand. I can't believe the lock broke and he hasn't noticed. He notices everything.

Bag on shoulder, I half fall through the window on to the flat roof over the kitchen and step more quickly than safety should allow on to the neighbour's roof which adjoins ours. I know they will be out all day and I can lower myself down into their flower bed. I'm hoping the guttering will hold my weight.

It doesn't. I pick myself out of the dahlias under the neighbour's kitchen window. The gutter is hanging down in limp failure. I hurt. My muddied jeans are covering grazed knees and I have wrenched my left shoulder. No time for pain or self-pity. Go.

Down the side of the neighbour's house. That way the camera over our front door won't pick me up. Oh God – Marcus is in his garden. Doesn't the man ever work? He is looking at me. He looks concerned. He's coming over. Shit.

"Laura – are you OK? What are you doing there?"

Think – quickly.

"I'm fine. I've just been doing a bit of gardening for Chris and Margaret and I slipped. Sorry, Marcus – got to run. Peter will be home soon and I need to get something for dinner."

Marcus hesitates. He doesn't look convinced. He's looking at my feet. The slippers!

"I know it's a bit weird. I've got the most awful bunions and these are the best things to wear at the moment."

"Oh – do you want a lift to the shop then? You won't want to walk."

This is getting worse.

"No really – that's fine, Marcus. It's only up the road and a walk is good for me sometimes. See you."

That's it. Quit while you're ahead. I'm running now – he'll be wondering how I can run with sore feet – oh, for goodness sake, it doesn't matter. Concentrate.

I'm heading for the nearest tube – Willesden Green. Change at Finchley Road. Providence is still helping – there's a Met Line train pulling in. Breathe.

***

I'm at King's Cross station. I need to say that again, to shout it inside my head. I'M AT KING'S CROSS STATION. But I don't feel free. I keep my head down and scurry along like I'm late for my own funeral. Sometimes I stop and look behind me – scanning the teeming commuters. He's not coming – he can't be coming. He has no idea where I am – how can he have?

I keep looking at my phone. I haven't turned it off. Why on earth not? Because he hasn't called. If he doesn't call, he doesn't know I've gone – logical really. He would call, wouldn't he? He would phone straight away to say where the hell are you? Wouldn't he? I won't answer it. I'll just know when he starts to work it out. I'm afraid.

I glance up at the departures board on the way to the ticket office – Aberdeen, Leeds, Cambridge, York. The names ebb and flow in my mind with the inconstancy of a mirage.

Queuing at the ticket office.

"Where to?"

Where to? Where do you go when your own personal handcart has already taken you to hell and back?

"Where to, Miss? You're holding up the queue."

I pluck a name from the places swirling in my head.

"What time is the York train?"

"15:08. It's on the board. If you want that one, you've got five minutes. You'd better run."

"OK – single, please."

You can't run in flip-flops. They're the ones I picked up on that stand near Willesden Green station. Why would you sell flip-flops in London? The slippers are in the bin. I'm carrying the flip-flops as I clamber into the nearest carriage of the waiting train and I hardly have time to take a seat before it starts to move. I'm going. I'm leaving London. I'm leaving Peter. Am I free?

I check my phone. Nothing. Maybe he's so busy at work he hasn't been able to look at his computer. No – stop wondering. He doesn't know where you are. He doesn't know.

***

"So now you know it all, all about my wasted life, my bastard of a husband . . . and why I'm running away. And I don't even know your name." Laura feels cleansed, emptied, as if telling all the sordid details of the past ten years has exposed them to the light and, vampire-like, they have withered to dust.

"It's Viv – my name is Viv." Laura clutches at the sympathy in Viv's eyes with the intensity of a drowning woman. Viv is clearly shaken, her voice hoarse and tense. Then Viv's phone buzzes loudly, shattering the moment. Laura stares as if her companion is holding a viper while Viv hesitates, before typing a brief response and dropping the phone in her bag with vehement decisiveness.

Another phone is buzzing. It takes a moment for Laura's

mind to register with dawning horror that it is her own – and she feels her stomach constrict as adrenaline floods her body. Reluctantly, she livens the screen. A text – from an unknown number. It can't be him. Maybe it's junk mail or something. She opens it.

I'm watching you.

She almost forgets to breathe.

"What is it?"

Laura stares at Viv like a rabbit in the headlights before mutely handing her the phone.

"He can't be watching you. He's just trying to frighten you. Classic scare tactics. He's just a bully."

But the screen hasn't even had time to go into sleep mode before it buzzes again. This time Viv opens it.

"Show me." Laura's voice is just a croak. With considerable misgiving, Viv hands the phone back.

Run, rabbit, run, rabbit, run, run, run.

And again. Words appear on the screen automatically.

You gave the farmer his fun, fun, fun.

Laura can't breathe. Again.

Bang, bang, bang, bang goes the farmer's gun.

She feels bile rise to her throat. The phone falls to the floor and Viv reaches down to retrieve it, pressing the off switch as she does so. She passes Laura a tissue.

"You have to get rid of this."

"How?" Laura's brain can only think in monosyllables.

"The toilet – that would do it. Drop it down the loo. He's just using scare tactics. He knows he's lost the fight and he can't bear it, so he's trying to control you from a distance."

"OK." All the strength has drained out of her.

"Look – I'll do it. Don't move."

Viv is back within two or three minutes.

"Lucky there was no queue. I dropped it down the pan but it wouldn't flush away, so I just put loads of loo paper on top of it. I've probably blocked the toilet, but who cares?"

Laura manages a sort of smile.

"I shouldn't have brought it with me. Why the hell did I do that?"

"Look, stop beating yourself up! You've been incredibly brave – but you must report this to the police as soon as you can. They'll have someone who can help you." Viv's hand tightens on Laura's arm to emphasise her words. "Very few people would have the courage to do what you've done. I've heard about these control freaks but I never thought I'd meet a victim. My God, I can't begin to imagine how awful it must have been for you." Viv turns to look out of the window for a moment and her eyes film over before the urgency of the situation reasserts itself.

Laura follows her gaze. Vast ploughed fields are disturbed only by the spire of a distant church.

"We've been here for ages. When do you think we'll get going?"

As if the driver had heard her, the speakers crackle to life.

**We apologise for the delay. The broken train has just been moved out of Huntingdon station. Due to the length of time we have been stationary, we will be making a short, unscheduled stop at Huntingdon. Any passengers wishing to alight there should prepare to do so.**

"That might help," Viv comments, a little too brightly.

"Really? How?" Laura is overwhelmed with bone-numbing weariness.

"Well, if your husband has found out, somehow, that you are on this train, he won't know you could have got off at Huntingdon, because the train isn't scheduled to stop there. So if he's driving to one of the stations on the way – which he won't be – you're in the clear. What do you think?"

Laura doesn't want to think. She wants to be led out of this moment without having to decide anything. Viv senses her indecision.

"Look, I'll get off with you. Maybe we can find a policeman or someone at the station who might be able to help you. You're going to be OK – you've had the guts to get this far."

The words are affirming, and Laura has been starved of affirmation for ten years. She pauses. Maybe she does have guts. Maybe she can take back the leading rein.

"Thank you."

As the train starts to move, murmurs of irritated relief can be heard throughout the carriage and a voice raised in complaint.

"About bloody time. Some idiot's blocked the toilet so I'll have to get off at the next station just to take a leak."

She and Viv exchange guilty looks.

**This is Huntingdon. Will passengers leaving the train here please make sure they have all their baggage with them.**

Clutching the handbag, Laura steps on to the platform with Viv following on. They are amongst the first off the train, but Laura still can't help casting a covert eye up and down the platform. Doors are opening and passengers are struggling with their luggage.

"Come on, let's see if we can find someone in authority." Viv's voice has taken on a controlling tone. Laura bristles. The woman has been more than a sounding board and her strength has rubbed off a little. But it seems wrong, somehow, to saddle her travelling companion with more of her problems and the last thing she needs is another person telling her what to do. She's beginning to realise she has started something she needs to see through alone.

"I need to go to the loo." Laura's voice sounds more confident than she feels. "You've been brilliant and I'm so very grateful. You've really helped me and given me the strength to sort this out. But I'll be fine now. Really. I've got to start making a future some time – it may as well be now. And you've got to get on and meet your friend."

"My friend? Oh yes, my friend." Viv grimaces but doesn't elaborate. "Are you absolutely sure you're going to be alright? I feel awful just leaving you. Promise me you'll get some help."

"I will, Viv. I will – promise." On impulse, Laura gives her a quick hug. "I've taken enough of your time already. Please go. You need to get to York – your friend will be wondering what's happened to you."

"He's going to have to wonder for a while longer. I'm going back to London. You keep telling me I've helped you – but you'll never know how much you've helped me. "

Laura watches puzzled as Viv crosses the footbridge to the other platform. The London train is pulling in and Laura catches a last glimpse of her counsellor as she boards it.

She doesn't allow herself more than a moment to wonder why Viv has changed her plans. She turns away towards the toilets. Even though she knows it's safe, she doesn't want to spend too long on the platform.

\*\*\*

Damn – there's a queue for the Ladies. I suppose there would be because we blocked the loo on the train.

"You look a bit desperate love."

It's a cleaning lady mopping the floor of the lobby. She's whispering at me.

"They should have more than one bog in here. Look, I've got a key to the disabled one here. It's down the other end of the platform. Why don't you use that? Leave the key there – I'll pick it up later."

I don't want to spend any more time here that I have

to. Yes, that'll help – but it means I have to go out on the platform. Got to hold myself together. Got to make another plan. I'm taking the key.

It's quite a long way to this disabled toilet. I'm cold. The wind's got up and I've only got a cardigan. Maybe I can pick up a coat somewhere. Finally. Here it is round the end of the building. I'm fiddling with the key now – it won't turn properly. OK. That's it . . .

What's that noise? What the hell is it? It's music. It is – not very loud, but clearly audible. I freeze. It's coming from my bag. And I recognise the tune.

Run, Rabbit, Run, Rabbit, Run, Run, Run . . .

I tear the bag open, breaking the clasp. The phone is down the toilet on its way to York. There's nothing in my bag except the emery board, the brush and the tissues, as well as the cash. I tip everything on the ground. The ringing goes on – louder, more insistent. I hold the bag to my ear, then feel around inside – something is vibrating. There's an object *inside* the lining – now I look, I can see the loose stitches where the seam has been ripped. There's another phone in there. I tear it out of its hiding place – it's a smartphone and it's alive in my hand. Then, it stops.

I am barely breathing. I bend down to pick up the contents of my bag, though my whole body is trembling.

"I'm watching you." The voice is barely a whisper. But I hear it.

My insides melt. He's here. He's found me. Like he always does. There's no escape, nowhere to hide. I can't turn round. I can't look at him, because then he'll be real. I don't want him to be real.

"I can't get by without my rabbit pie . . . "

I feel his hand on my arm, dragging me to my feet and forcing me into the disabled toilet. He thrusts me towards the back wall, where I stand pinioned, face pressed against the rough plaster. I can smell the reek of stale urine from the floor.

He's going to kill me. I know it. He's come here to kill me. He used to tell me they shot cowards in the back when they deserted. Shouting is no use. I'm right at the other end of the now-empty platform. I try it anyway, but what emerges is no more than a croak. I try to free my arm but it's up my back.

He hisses in my ear.

"I knew where you were all along, you know. You're so useless you couldn't even run away and get it right."

"How?" I manage.

"The phone. You wouldn't understand because you're a technical imbecile, aren't you? Ever heard of GPS? No? Well it's on the phone."

"I got rid of the phone."

"Oh that one – that was just a ploy. The other one was the real business. I was bored, Laura. Bored with your miserable face, bored with your scrawny body, bored, bored, bored. You're a frigid cow, you know. A man needs a bit of fun – a bit of something to stimulate the mind – so I decided to play a little game."

I can't believe what I'm hearing.

"You don't imagine I didn't know you stole my money, do you? You think I don't count it? How did you think I wouldn't know what you were doing when you hid it in the boxing? And you didn't even wonder about the bag, did you? Do you like the smartphone? I bought it specially. And I think you should thank me for making it so easy for you – I even broke the window latch so you could get out quickly.

"I was watching all the time, Laura. I like to watch you, even when you're running away. You run and I follow.

104

You're mine, you see. You belong to me."

"You followed me?"

"All the way, Laura. First on the phone and then on the train."

"You were on the train?" Can you be incredulous and hopeless at the same time?

"Caught up with the train at Stevenage. Thought I wasn't going to make it, but Lady Luck was running with me. You were looking out of the window. I walked right past you and sat down the far end of the carriage. I saw your new buddy take the old phone to the bog and come back without it." He wrenches my arm up my back viciously.

"So you tracked me on the other phone in my bag . . . "

"Got it in one, genius. Child's play. Rig the bag, give it to you and set up your 'escape'. I didn't really think you had the guts to go through with it. But you've surprised me. I hadn't made a plan for this bit. I have now, though." His voice darkened.

"You utter bastard."

"Oh no, Laura. You don't want to us to end up with those words between us, do you? After all I've given to you, all that undivided attention? I worshipped you." I can feel his body pressed into my back, rigid with tension. I become aware that his madness is now fuelled by sexual arousal. Help me.

His voice is hoarse. "I know you still love me Laura. I know it. I need to hear you say it. Because marriage is for life. And for eternity. You promised. Say it!"

What's he talking about – marriage is for eternity? Oh my God, no. Of course – he's going to kill us both – so I can never get away till the end of time. I am paralysed with horror.

"Say it." His lips are against my ear. I say nothing and

wait. My knees are giving way, my head is swimming. It's coming . . .

No – why is his hand loosening on my forearm? Without warning, he lets it fall. He must be reaching for a weapon . . . I whirl round. He has backed away, right hand raised to his throat. His breath is coming in shallow gasps. Unsteadily, he leans back against the wall, then slides down it until he is on the floor, head wedged against the toilet. Is this just another ruse to prolong the torture? I can't believe what I am seeing.

Believe it. One side of his mouth has dropped and his complexion is suffused with blood. His right arm lies across his body at an angle and his hand dangles uselessly over his ribcage. His left arm twitches. No, this is genuine. He was so enraged, yet so contained that his body has rebelled. I know these symptoms. He made me read enough leaflets after his dad died. He was paranoid about it. Face, arm, speech, telephone – FAST – I had to repeat the mantra over and over till I was saying it in my sleep.

He's had a stroke. I am looking at his eyes, flooded as they are with panic, with fear. I recognise both, because they are old friends. They are pleading with me. A distorted sound escapes, but speech has deserted him. He is helpless. For the love of God – he's helpless and I am not. I am not helpless. I pick up the small phone from the floor. My finger hovers over the nine. I press it once, then . . . not a second time. No, not a second time. I watch as the flicker of relief in his eyes turns to confusion, then desperation. Yes, I watch. I am the watcher now.

Very slowly, I back away from him. He is grunting and slobbering, his better hand trying to reach towards me. There is a bluish tinge around his lips and his breath is rasping. Do I feel pity? Do I?

Without haste, I drop the phone in the waste paper bin. I cover it with paper towels, so that when they empty it, they won't even notice.

I open the door and turn to take one final look at the contorted face, the terrified eyes – then, very gently, I close the door. I take my time putting the key in the lock. I can't hear the laboured breathing any more.

Now it is his turn. The key grates in the lock. I hope he can still hear my footsteps as I walk away.

# Carpe diem
## by Chris Payne

MOST people saw it as a penance. For Matt, though, the local careers fair was a source of satisfaction. Every year, the HR manager at Booth & Bayne went on the prowl for someone to look after the stall for an evening. No one ever volunteered. "A night full of sweaty kids and anxious parents? No thanks," his colleagues scoffed. "The kids only want the free pens and the parents want a guaranteed career. Either way you get no conversation and no respect. There are better ways to spend an evening," they concluded.

Matt would smile in outward agreement but, secretly, he *liked* the fairs. He felt important as he stood beside the table filled with corporate literature, answering questions on project management with considered judgement. Looking like an expert at not yet thirty. The eager sixth-formers who approached him reminded him of himself, ten years earlier. It was at a fair like this that Booth & Bayne had thrown him the lifeline that let him stay in York. He'd approached their table, with his projected 'A' levels and a list of endorsements from his boarding-school teachers, and had been accepted as an intern. He'd never had to live in London again.

This rose-tinted perspective on the careers fair wasn't acceptable in the office, though, so Matt kept up the required show of disdain when he was finally approached. He'd been aware for a few minutes that Hannah, the HR manager, was standing near his desk but he feigned absorption in the spreadsheet on his screen and only looked around, with a simulated start, when she gave a discreet cough. She laid an advert for the fair on his desk.

"You've done such a good job of it before, you know you have. The ones you've brought in on internships have actually done some work: not like the ones Derek brought in last year," Hannah wheedled. Lowering her voice, she glanced around before continuing. "We just can't have Derek doing it on his own. It's his age . . . you know . . . he's a bit past it when it comes to talking to the next generation. They look at him and they see their dads. But they look at you and see someone they can actually relate to, something they could aspire to be. Plus, since you came in on an internship yourself, they realise that it works, it's not just slave labour we're after. It can lead to a career. It makes them realise that project management is a job for a normal person."

Matt snorted. "Is it? Do you think?" He slid open a desk drawer and pulled out his diary and a buff-coloured folder. "What's the date, again?"

"April 14$^{th}$. Are you free?"

Matt opened the diary slightly, holding the cover at an angle so that Hannah couldn't see the number of blank pages inside. "Hmm, yes. I think I can make it work," he said briskly, snapping the diary shut. He turned to the folder and showed her the list inside. "Here's the project plan I used last time. Has anything changed?"

Hannah glanced at the list and lifted her eyebrows. "Where did this come from? It looks really . . . comprehensive."

Matt flushed slightly, saying, "It's just a little checklist I put together to make sure the fair ran smoothly when I did it before. I like to have things organised in advance." He laughed ruefully. "I'm not a project manager by accident, you know! My father always used to say *Fail to prepare? Then prepare to fail.*" He slipped the folder back into his drawer, adding, "It's a quote from Benjamin Franklin."

Hannah laughed in answer. "I guess the planning gene runs in your family! You were born to be a planner."

It was a Wednesday so, on his way home that evening, Matt stopped for a takeaway fish and chip supper. When he reached his flat, he snapped on the light and laid the wrapped and lightly steaming parcel on the tray he'd set out ready on the hall table that morning. He paused a moment, struck by his own preparations. Hannah's words rang again in his ears and he shrugged. "Perhaps I *was* born to be a planner," he muttered as he slipped off his shoes.

Come April 14th, Matt placed his laptop in the top of a box full of pop-up banners and glossy leaflets. Arriving early at the school hall, he found the room in chaos. Anxious teachers were struggling to lay out the room in to some sort of order, while many of the tables were still stacked against the wall. The exhibitors were all funnelled into a small vestibule to keep them out of the way. Matt eased into a corner and put his box of supplies on the floor. He gazed idly out of the rain-spattered window into the car park, full of harried businessmen busily emptying their boots of boxes just like his.

A small white van turned into the car park, a bit too sharply, and braked noisily outside the door. Matt watched a woman of about his age climb out and call over to some teachers who were loitering around the corner, away from the manual labour of the hall. They ambled over to her van and, together, started unloading large, square packages. Even through the window, Matt could hear the ring of the woman's laughter as she threw her head back in response to something one of the teachers said. Then, behind him, the door to the hall opened and the exhibitors were beckoned in. Matt shook his head and lifted his box, ready to create his Booth & Bayne shop window.

All through the evening that same laugh seemed to cut through the hubbub in the room. Matt could see that, in the laughing woman's corner, there were no laptops or leaflets: large canvases, which must have come from the square packages he'd glimpsed in the car park, were propped up against the wall before a table full of glittering knick-knacks. Through the throng of students, Matt caught an occasional glimpse of someone perched on the edge of the table, rather than standing behind it, wearing a flowing multi-coloured skirt and crowned with a cloud of wild, curly hair. Her table appeared to be advertising the local College of Art and Design: some freak of planning must have placed her artist's table in a hall full of accountants, project managers and lawyers.

The sixth-formers who ventured here were the bespectacled and the bookish, who Matt thought would bypass her bright colours with no more than an uncomfortable glance. But, like moths to a flame, they fluttered in front of her all through the evening, obscuring Matt's gaze as they crowded round her table with their eager questions.

Part-way through the evening Matt made an excuse to his colleague and wandered round the room, nodding to business acquaintances standing glumly beside their corporate colours. As he neared the artist's table he realised that the glittering objects covering the table were snowglobes, each holding a different scene: snowmen, dragons, fairies, cities, pyramids. Some swirled with white flakes; others held a shimmering dust in millions of colours. Matt gave up pretending not to look and gaped openly. He felt he had to touch one for himself.

He approached the table and selected one from the middle row, its glass un-smudged by fingerprints. He lifted it and peered inside at the small figure, standing with bow and arrow poised. As he swirled the globe in a circle, gently, to lift the dust, a low voice spoke from close beside him. "It needs a big shake. It's been sitting still for a long time and it takes some energy to wake it up." Matt turned, and his eyes met the dark gaze of the woman whose laugh he'd been hearing all evening. Her eyes shone like pebbles under water, their colour as dark as the pupils. As his eyes locked on her single, solid gleam, he felt a physical shock in the pit of his stomach. *This is it*, he remembered thinking. *This is what people mean when they say* 'Love at first sight'.

When the fair ended and all the stands were being packed away, when the only person in the room not connected with an exhibition was the caretaker disconsolately pushing a broom around, Matt returned to her corner and invited her out for the rest of the evening. He reeled home that night, his mind swirling like the snow globe and her name, Gemma, ringing in his ears with the music of her laugh.

Matt woke the next morning to a text message inviting him to a picnic in the park that evening. All day he couldn't concentrate on his work, with Gemma's face drifting between him and the screen. Promptly at five he pushed back his chair and left the office at a run. As he entered the park gates, he could see Gemma sitting on a blanket spread under an oak tree. At the sight of her he felt as if the lightness in his heart could float him across to join her.

In the following weeks, Matt responded to Gemma's daily text messages drawing him to new activities. Suddenly he was pulled into a whirlpool of gallery viewings, film screenings and murder mysteries held in the depths of the Shambles. He spent each lunchtime wandering the streets near his office, happily imagining the evening ahead. His colleagues remarked that they'd never seen him smile so much.

The first night Gemma visited his flat she looked around in disbelief. "How long have you lived here, Matt?"

"Seven years. I moved in right after I finished my

114

apprenticeship at Booth & Bayne, once I could get a mortgage."

"OK, and let me guess," Gemma continued. "You haven't done a single thing to it. In. All. That. Time?"

Matt took a slow look around, not sure what Gemma meant. He saw what he always saw: the smooth grey walls with the trim white skirting at the bottom; the shining grey carpet that put him in mind of the sea.

"What's wrong with it?" he asked, bewildered.

"What's *wrong* with it? Where's your stuff? Where are your pictures? Where are *you*, Matt?" Gemma had shaken her head and laughed. "I can see I'm going to have my work cut out!"

On her next visit, she brought the snow globe with its miniature Eros and placed it on the hall table, sending the fish and chip tray back to the kitchen. Each visit after that she brought a canvas, a weaving or an ornament and she stood back, directing Matt where each object should be placed. After her fourth visit, she never went home again.

The second bedroom became a studio for her work. Suddenly every pale wall was covered with splashes of colour: Gemma's art was hung or draped over every surface. The kitchen, formerly home to takeaway containers and ready-meal wrappers, was now filled with the clatter of pans and the smell of spices.

Matt's empty diary remained unfilled: Gemma didn't believe in planning ahead. But one appointment was fixed: the Friday night pub crawl in the company of her art-teacher colleagues. One evening just before Christmas, when Gemma was at the bar, her closest friend leaned liquidly into Matt. "You know, you've been the best thing ever for Gem," Erin slurred.

Matt raised his eyebrows. "*Ever*? Really?"

Erin nodded vehemently and poked him in the chest. "Yes! Ever! She's always been happy, but she's never found a guy she liked. Most of them have all been kind of flaky, you know? Never turning up when they said. You don't do that."

Matt smiled ruefully and sipped his pint. "No, I don't do that," he agreed.

"Exactly!" declared Erin loudly. She set her own glass down carefully. "And Gemma's kind of flaky too, right? But in a good way. And if you get a flaky girl and a flaky guy, what do you get?" she stared at him belligerently and waited for an answer.

Matt thought a moment. "Umm . . . flakes?" he ventured.

Erin punched his arm. "Exactly! Two flakes make a giant flake! Not good." She leaned back and blinked owlishly. Matt recognised the signs and thought reluctantly that they'd be taking Erin back to the flat again tonight. Then her eyes sprang open. "But a flake and a rock . . . that's OK!" she declared, closing her eyes briefly before opening them again as she clarified her point. "You're the rock."

"Thanks, Erin," Matt grinned. He glanced at the bar, where Gemma was just turning around with a glass in each hand. Catching his eye, she beamed and raised and lowered her eyebrows rapidly, trying to convey some urgent message to do with the drinks. Matt raised his glass to her and kept his eyes fixed on her face as she approached. He wasn't sure if he agreed with Erin's description but he agreed with her assessment. Whatever it was about him and Gemma together, it just worked.

After ten blissful months together, Gemma announced she had a surprise. One of her colleagues at the College had a holiday cottage free for the February half-term.

"She needs someone to go and open it up for her," Gemma explained, excitedly, as she cooked dinner. "She's renting it in March and she needs someone to go up and switch the heating on, air the beds, stuff like that: she won't have time to do it all before her renters are due and she can't get up there in half-term herself. So I said we'd do it."

When they arrived at the cottage, they pushed open its

heavy wooden door to a cold that was more intense inside the house than outside. "When was she last up here?" Matt asked.

"Before Christmas, she said," replied Gemma, vaguely, through chattering teeth. "Can we find some firewood? She didn't warn me it would be this cold!"

With the help of the fire, they were finally able to discard their jackets and start toasting marshmallows. They had a perfect week; each day they tramped through the countryside, marvelling at the fishermen stolidly pulling their catches from the River Wharfe without a thought for the weather. They played board games in front of the fireplace and warmed each other through the night under the chill duvets. On their last evening they sat in front of the fireplace and toasted each other with mugs of hot chocolate, Gemma curled up against Matt's side.

Then she spoke, still looking at the fire. "Matt?"

"Yes?"

"I've been wanting to ask you something. Do you mind?"

"Of course not. You know you can ask me anything."

"Why do you never talk about your father?" Matt stirred slightly and Gemma lifted her head. "I don't mind, but it just seems . . . odd. Even at Christmas you didn't go to see him. I know you don't like your stepmother, but do you not get on with your dad at all?"

Matt paused. "It's not that, exactly. It's not that we don't get *on*. I just have nothing to say to him. Every conversation we have has this big subtext running under it and I can't hear what he's saying for all the shouting in my head."

"What do you mean?" asked Gemma.

"Well, you remember I told you about how my mother died when I was ten and my father remarried?"

Gemma nodded.

"And you know his new wife is nice enough and everything, but it was the timing. He married her less than a year after

117

my mum died. And she – his new wife, Rosalina – she used to be our *au pair*. She'd walk me home from school, make me sandwiches, help me with my homework. But I never imagined that she and my dad ever had any more contact than when he handed over her weekly money . . . I just felt so stupid when they told me."

"You were only a child," consoled Gemma. "And it's a long time ago, right?"

"Yes, I was only ten! I didn't even understand what had happened. I was supposed just to accept straight away that she'd be moving into my dad's room, that she'd join us at dinner, that she'd just always be there. It made me sick, physically sick, but I couldn't do anything about it.

"They hit me with a double whammy: first they told me they were getting married, then they said they'd be sending me to boarding school. My dad said it would be easier for me to be part of the school community. I just felt that I . . . that I wasn't wanted." Gemma stroked his face and Matt stared into the fire for a few moments. "It was the textbook wrong way to deliver news, really. It was my eleventh birthday when they told me." He sipped his hot chocolate and gave a small laugh.

"It was funny, when you think about it. It was my first birthday without my mother. She'd always been the birthday one; it was always the summer holidays when my dad was at work. Mum and I would do something together, usually something outside. She loved being outside. So we'd get pedalos in Hyde Park, or go mud-larking down by the Thames. And, wherever we went, we'd collect a souvenir of the day like a pebble or a pine cone. Something natural, anyway. And I'd bring it home, carefully, in my shorts-pocket. I couldn't wait to show Dad when he got home, to tell him what Mum and I had been doing all day. He'd act interested, and he kept all the souvenirs lined up in a row on his study window-sill." Matt shifted slightly and Gemma settled herself against him again, listening.

"So, on the morning of my birthday, I'd just finished reading *Harry Potter* and I woke up thinking about it, how on *his* eleventh birthday he'd had a letter delivered by an owl, telling him he was a wizard and was going away to school."

Matt glanced down at Gemma. "I actually looked out my window, just in case. Not an owl in sight. And, when I went downstairs, there were all these presents wrapped all funny. Dad wasn't much with the wrapping, but he did use a lot of tape to make up for it. And although Mum wasn't there, and it was all wrong, I thought at least it was him and me and he was trying to make it a birthday."

He paused. "So Dad was there but so was Rosalina which wasn't normal, not in the morning. She was standing over by the window-sill, picking up my souvenirs. Just picking them up and putting them down again, not doing any harm, really . . . but I didn't like seeing my things in her hands."

Gemma nodded. "I can imagine! Maybe she didn't realise?"

"Maybe not . . . Anyway I started to open the presents, then Rosalina moved over to sit next to Dad. I remember noticing that she was sitting really close to him. And Dad said in this really hearty voice, like it was an extra birthday treat, that Rosalina did such a good job of looking after me that she was going to be my new mother from now on."

Gemma sat up so suddenly her hot chocolate nearly spilled. "Your *new mother*? He came right out and said that?"

Matt nodded, tears standing in his eyes. "I didn't know what to do, Gem. I was only eleven. Barely. But I felt so sick and I had no words. I just ran from the study up to my bedroom, and I howled and howled. I felt like my insides were coming out. Eventually Dad came upstairs and said he was sorry I'd reacted like that. He told me I'd missed the other part of his news, that he and Rosalina had decided it would be best for me to go to a boarding secondary school and I'd be starting there next month, at the end of the summer holidays.

"So I got my wish, in a way. I got my escape to school. Just no owls, and no magic."

Gemma put down her mug and encircled Matt in her arms. "That's such a horrible way to treat a child. You were still grieving and he sent you away?"

Matt nodded. "As I got older, it was the disloyalty I couldn't get over. I mean, Rosalina had known my mother! Was Dad carrying on with her even when Mum was sick? I don't know . . . he said not. When I was about fourteen we had a massive argument and I threw that in his face. You can imagine . . . But I don't know, I guess they just wanted to be alone. Going home was torture. I spent all my holiday time at the library, studying. I just wasn't able to stand being in the same room as him. As *them*. As soon as I finished sixth-form I enrolled on the apprenticeship at Booth & Bayne, got my qualifications and I've been there ever since."

"And you don't write, you don't call, you don't visit . . . nothing?"

"I send a Christmas card . . . I have manners." Matt laughed with no humour. "No, nothing. There's just nothing there. He made his choice and it didn't include me. I just don't think of myself as having family any more."

Gemma gazed up at Matt and stroked the side of his face with her hand. "You have me," she said, gently, and lifted her face to kiss him.

That was the moment when Matt knew he wanted to be with Gemma for ever.

After the holiday, when they returned to York, he knew he needed a plan. On his first day back at work, he opened up his computer and started up a new spreadsheet. *Project Jewel* he called it, smiling to himself at the pun. If Gemma was to have the most romantic proposal ever, he needed to plan it perfectly.

*Begin with the end in mind*, Matt muttered as he began to enter data in the cells. It was another of his father's favourite sayings. It seemed no matter how hard he tried to shake off everything from his past, the pithy phrases stuck in his mind. He carefully labelled the columns with everything he could think of that he'd need: *Wording, Ring, Venue, Transport, Accessories, Music.*

First of all, though, *Timing*. When would he ask her? Matt smiled as he thought about the day that they had met: April 14th, the first anniversary of the careers fair, would be the perfect date. He carefully entered April 14th on the project plan as the target date. That gave him about six weeks to plan it.

For the next couple of weeks, he spent every lunch-time searching the internet for examples of perfect marriage proposals. Gemma deserved the best. People had shared all sorts of details about their own experiences, giving him good ideas of what to do and, more importantly, what not to. Apparently hiding the ring in a dessert was fraught with danger, not to mention the hygiene issues. Matt made notes, and kept searching.

One item on the spreadsheet, though, kept coming into his mind. *Ring*. This was both the easiest and hardest part of the whole programme: he knew precisely which ring he would need, and he knew where to get it. But in order to get it, he'd have to break the silence and contact his father again. Matt sighed, scrolling through his contacts list for the email address that was enclosed in each year's Christmas card. For the last seven Decembers he'd checked that it was still the same, but he hadn't used it until now. He opened up a new email and thought for a moment about what to say. How do you write a note to your closest living relative who is also a stranger? And what to call him? He sighed again and flexed his fingers on the keyboard. His father had always said not to beat around the bush, so he might as well get straight to the point. No small talk, no false interest in his health. He couldn't bring himself to type *Dad* so left the message without a salutation.

As you know, Mum left me her engagement ring
in her will. Could you please post it to me? My
address is still the same.
Thanks,
Matt

He didn't expect a reply quickly, but he was surprised:
a response pinged in within the hour.

Matthew,
Thank you for your message. It would be better
if you collected the ring yourself. Thursday 19th
March would be convenient for me and Rosalina.
We will be home all morning.
Charles

*First names, then,* thought Matt. *No more Dad.* There was
nothing for it; he'd have to go there in person. Deep down
he knew the old man was right; you couldn't use Royal Mail
to deliver a valuable ring. He sighed, wondering how he was
going to manage this without Gemma knowing. He'd have to
work it into his daily schedule; he could get to London and
back in a day and she'd never suspect a thing.

The night before he was due to collect the ring, as they were
getting ready for bed, Matt casually said, "Gemma, I'm not
coming back from my run tomorrow."

"What do you mean, not coming back? You're going straight
into work?"

"Yes . . . I've got to finish that presentation so I thought I'd
cut my run short and go straight into the office. I can have a
quick shower there and get the whole thing finished before
Derek gets in. Then I won't need to stay late, either."

"Oh, OK then. But don't work too hard!" Gemma kissed
him good night and slipped into the bed.

It was easier than Matt had thought. His morning run always followed the same route. Into the city through Walmgate Bar, then across the River Foss before diving into the warren of small streets loved by the tourists. At this time of day, he could run through the streets like a medieval message boy, unworried by traffic or crowds. *It's hard to believe*, Matt thought as he ran, *that in only an hour's time these streets will be thronged with early commuters and snap-happy holiday-makers.* Today, instead of turning off Micklegate and closing the loop back to home, he carried on straight to Queen Street before swinging right and running up to the station entrance. His foot splashed in a puddle and startled a brace of pigeons which flew away from each other in a hurried confusion of rustling feathers, like lovers startled from a clandestine embrace.

It was surprising how little time passed before he was standing in front of his father's home. For years Matt had cited the distance and inconvenience of travel as reasons why he could never get back for holidays yet here he was, just a few hours after he'd left Gemma that morning, transported back to his childhood. The house was smaller than he remembered. The three red-brick storeys no longer loomed forbiddingly but seemed cosier, more homely. Matt stood with his back to the wrought-iron railings of the gardens opposite and stared up at the building he'd once known so well. *Home is where the heart is*, he recalled his father saying; but Matt's heart had died from this house when his mother had. His gaze travelled upwards and picked out a small diamond wink of light where the weak morning sun struck a top-floor window. It reminded him of evenings on his window-seat, flashing his lonely torch beam out into the night in the hope that someone would see his signal.

Matt pulled himself back to the present and glanced at his watch. He crossed the road to climb the steps to the shining black front door. Drawing a deep breath, he pressed his finger firmly on the doorbell. The door immediately sprang open and his father stood there.

Matt's first thought, in some disbelief, was *He's getting old*. His father had stayed the same in his mind all the time: the stiff back, the neatly combed dark hair, the steel blue tie. Now the hair was greying at the temples and he wore small glasses. He was wearing a business shirt with a dark brown cardigan over it, but no tie. How old was he now? Sixty? Had he retired? Matt couldn't remember.

"Matthew. It's good to see you," his father said, neutrally, standing back to let Matt in. They stood, awkwardly, in the hall for a moment, unsure whether a handshake or hug was needed. In the end they did neither. Charles turned to open the drawing room door, saying "Rosalina is in here." Behind his back, Matt made a face at himself in the hall mirror before composing his features to greet his stepmother.

She was standing by the mantelpiece. Her arm was draped uncomfortably along it, below the mirror, in a position she'd clearly chosen to appear relaxed. Matt wondered how long she'd been standing there.

"Matt, it's good to see you," she exclaimed, her Spanish accent still evident even after all the time she had lived in England. She walked towards him with her hands outstretched, and Matt lifted his laptop bag protectively in front of his body. He sat down abruptly on the nearest chair, smiling and nodding as if in a normal greeting while avoiding any possibility of touching her. She wisely dropped her hands to her sides and stepped back.

"I'll get some coffee. Or would you rather have tea?" she asked.

"Neither, thanks," said Matt quickly. "I can't stay long. I need to get back to York."

"Oh, but we thought . . . " she began, then broke off with a glance at his father. "I'll get the coffee."

She closed the door behind her and the room went quiet.

Matt waited, but his father continued to gaze out of the window. Matt was determined not to speak first so, unwillingly, he began to look round the room.

It hadn't changed since he'd last seen it, ten years ago, when he'd returned to pack up his room for the final time. Then, as now, he'd sat in this chair waiting for his father to speak. Rosalina had perched on the yellow love seat, wringing her hands as Matt's father tried to persuade him to forget this idea of an apprenticeship in York.

Matt's gaze travelled around the room and stopped on his father. He was startled to realise that his father was carefully picking up the row of ten birthday souvenirs, one by one. He spoke so softly that Matt had to lean forward to hear him.

"She – in fact, we – hoped you'd stay for lunch with us."

"No, D- . . . Charles, no. I can't. I have to be back to York this evening. I haven't told Gemma I'm here because I want the ring to be a surprise when it's time to use it."

"Does she know about us?" his father asked, still not turning to face Matt.

The silence in the room seemed to swell until Matt finally said, "I've told her all about my life, yes."

Charles replaced the final souvenir, a shiny pebble Matt remembered plucking from the muddy banks of the Thames. He could still hear the satisfying sucking sound the mud made as he pulled the pebble free before it re-formed to a smooth surface.

The door swung open and Rosalina entered with a tray holding a silver coffeepot and several cups. "I brought some for you, too, Matt," she said diffidently. "Just in case."

Matt smiled and nodded, realising that if he was going to maintain the veneer of politeness, he couldn't just run away. He accepted the cup of coffee, with thanks, and took a sip. The room was silent. He sipped his drink again. "Busy at work?" his father finally offered.

"Yes, thank you," Matt replied. He took another sip of his coffee and cast his eyes around the room for something he could safely comment on. "That picture," he offered lamely, "is it new?"

Charles and Rosalina's eyes followed his glance with relief, followed by surprise. "Quite a few years old now," Rosalina explained.

"New since your last visit," Charles added.

The silence fell again and Matt sipped his coffee. When would it cool enough for him to finish it and get out of here?

Rosalina shifted slightly in her seat and Matt noticed that her leg was pressed firmly against his father's, as if offering him support. He looked away again, flushing. He remembered her sitting in that same position, on that same love seat, during the worst conversation of his life.

Matt shoved himself urgently up from his seat, coffee slopping into the saucer. He put it down, roughly, on the low table and said, "Look, this isn't working. I just have to go. Can I have the ring, please?"

His father froze in the act of sipping from his cup. He glanced at Rosalina, then back to Matt, and sighed. "I hoped . . . I had some things . . . I guess you're right. Perhaps now isn't the time." He rose, crossed the room to a small bureau and pulled out a padded envelope, securely sealed with tape. "I had the ring cleaned and valued," he said. "The documentation is in the envelope with it. I hope your young lady likes it and that it brings her – and you – as much happiness as it did to your mother and me."

Matt tucked the envelope into his bag alongside his computer. The words stuck in his throat, briefly, but he managed to say, "Thank you."

"It's alright, Matthew, you know you can always come here. For anything."

Matt turned to step out of the door but his impetus to move

was halted by his father's words: "And you know, we'd love to meet her. Your betrothed. To be."

Matt turned, and saw in his father's eyes a vulnerability he had never expected to see there. He couldn't bring himself to answer, so he parried the question. "I'll let you know when anything changes . . . I haven't even asked her yet." And without another word he turned and hurried down the steps.

King's Cross station was very familiar: it was where he'd departed from each term to head north to his boarding school. Today he had some time before his 15:08 train so he gave in to a private indulgence and sought out platform 9¾, the place where Harry Potter's train had left for each trip to Hogwart's. When his father and Rosalina had brought him to the station each term Matt had felt like Harry, straining to be away from them and into his new life.

Matt smiled to see the baggage trolley pushed half-way through the brick wall at the place where the wizarding platform was supposed to be, then turned to find his own more prosaic departure point. He boarded the train, found his seat and checked his watch. Right on schedule: he would be back in York at five-thirty, which would get him home at the regular time. Gemma wouldn't suspect a thing.

As the train began moving from the station, Matt took out his laptop to update the project tracker. He marked the *Ring* column *Complete* and coloured the spreadsheet cell green.

The plan was progressing nicely: he'd booked Middlethorpe Hall for the following month and a hired limousine would pick them up in the morning and take them there. He had booked the best bedroom for the night and chosen a spa treatment for Gemma. It was going to be the perfect proposal and there was only a little more than three weeks to go.

Matt's phone buzzed with a text message. He pulled out the phone and looked at the screen: it was from Derek in the office.

Hope mission was successful. I'm off tomorrow morning as

127

am having late night tonight. I've left the project update on your desk. Tx – Derek

He texted back a brief acknowledgement and wondered for a moment about Derek's 'late night'. Derek never went out in the evenings, as far as Matt knew. He was single and seemed to have few hobbies or friends: most Mondays he would regale Matt at length with the progress he'd made with cataloguing his vast collection of Motown records. *It's a shame he's never met the love of his life*, Matt thought.

He closed the spreadsheet and rested his head back on the seat. It had been a long day of travelling but at least he'd managed to get the ring without arguing with his father. He drifted into a doze, then jerked awake at a hissing noise as the train slowed down. Suddenly the tannoy speaker above his head crackled slightly and a voice announced:

**We apologise for the delay. A train ahead of us has broken down. We will keep you informed, but expect to continue our journey shortly.**

All through the carriage came the sound of muted sighs and tuts, the normal British chorus of response to transport issues. Matt checked his watch. As long as they weren't stuck for very long he would be home in time and Gemma wouldn't realise he hadn't been at work. He turned his attention back to the computer but realised that his doze had been long enough for it to go to sleep. He shut the lid and lifted his bag to put it away.

As he did so, Matt felt the bulky envelope his father had given him. There was no one sitting near him, so he could usefully get the ring out of the envelope and check that it looked as he remembered. He used his key to slit the strong tape that secured the envelope.

Inside was wedged a navy velvet ring box. Matt set it carefully on the tray table in front of him, lifted the lid and smiled. The ring was exactly as he'd remembered it: a row of three small seed pearls banked either side by tiny garnets and diamonds in an alternating pattern. It glowed softly in the harsh lights of the train carriage, looking full of serenity and promise. He imagined Gemma's slim brown finger being lit by its beauty.

Matt admired it for a moment then, glancing around in case anyone was watching him, snapped the box shut and tucked it back into the envelope. He drew out the paperwork inside: there were two other flat envelopes, one sealed and one open. He peeped inside the unsealed flap: there was the valuation his father had mentioned. Curious, he turned over the other envelope and saw his name, written in the strong, spiky capital letters his father always favoured.

The speaker above his head crackled again and a voice intoned:

**We regret to inform you that we will be unable to move on for up to an hour. Engineers are working as fast as possible to clear the other train from the line. Meanwhile, we ask for your patience. The buffet car is open.**

The sighs and tuts were louder this time, and Matt could hear the querulous sound of young children from the seats behind him. A few people began to move rapidly in the direction of the buffet car, hoping to beat the inevitable queues. A woman nearby looked impatient, her every movement showing intolerance for the situation, and she shoved her way down the aisle with her coat and bag thrust in front of her.

Matt returned his attention to the envelope from his father. He couldn't imagine what the old man could want to say to him. He shuffled in to a new sitting position: at least he had the two seats to himself.

Inside the envelope was a letter, written in the same strong, dark hand:

Dear Matthew,

I am writing you this letter as I am not confident I will be able to speak these words to you in person. We meet so seldom and each time we do it is uncomfortable for both of us. I want you to know how much I regret that.

I was delighted to hear you wanted your mother's ring, since I assume you intend to propose to your girlfriend. I wish you success and joy in your relationship, as much as I have been fortunate enough to have in both of mine.

I know that you have never forgiven me for marrying Rosalina and that you felt that I was disloyal to your mother's memory for doing so. I am so sorry for having caused you so much pain. I can never make amends, but perhaps I can explain.

The 15 years I had with your mother were the happiest of my life. Once she was gone I was bereft and couldn't see a way forward: how would I manage on my own, how could I care for you?

Boarding school seemed the best way to give you a solid schooling environment that would fit with my long working hours. My own experience as a boarder made me stronger and more self-sufficient: it gave an extra "family" beyond what I had at home in the holidays.

Then Rosalina seemed the answer to my prayers for re-building a happy home life. When I realised I had feelings for her I decided, for once, not to follow the advice I always gave you about preparing and planning carefully. Instead, I followed your mother's philosophy of carpe diem and I seized the day, asking Rosalina to marry me. She'd known your mother, and she could honour her memory without competing with it. Best of all she knew you, and she cared for you.

But I was wrong to think that I could re-create a happy family so quickly. I know now that by my mistake I lost you, just after I'd lost your mother.

I do not regret the comfort Rosalina brought to me. I love her but she knows that it is not the love I had for your mother, the love that brought you to my life. I can never bring your mother back, and I can never right the wrong I did to you. Rosalina and I have been happy, but that happiness is not what I had hoped it would be when I thought it would include you. If I'd realised that you would turn from me so strongly, I would never have acted as I did.

When I look at you, I see your mother again. You have her bright optimism and her curiosity about the world. She would have loved to see that you are embarking on this next phase in your life.

I want to wish you joy as you seize your day. You deserve to know the happiness of a loving relationship and I hope you have a delightful future with your young lady.

Your father,
Charles

Matt's eyes misted in tears. *Seize the day*, he thought. He glanced down at the computer tucked into his bag and thought about his project plan, how he'd been planning for his perfect proposal. *But what does it really matter?* he wondered. *The romance is in our life together, not in the trappings that go around it.*

He picked up his phone and tapped out a text to Gemma: Delayed on train but home soon: long story. Will you be in tonight? I have something important to ask you. Xx

The reply came back immediately: Train? Yes am home. Can't wait to see you. Love you! Xxxxxx G

Matt put the phone away with a smile. *Carpe diem*: tonight would be the night.

# In your own best interest

by Emma Dark

PRIMAVERA sat on the train with her head in her hands. She'd been in plenty of time to catch the 15:08 from King's Cross. She was going to see Sheila, her one and only friend, who had moved to Peterborough a few years back. This was their once-a-month knees-up. Prim, as she was known, had thought they would be having a celebratory pint but things hadn't worked out. She'd thought the meeting with the social worker would be a walk in the park – how wrong she was. So now it would be a solacing pint and, as always, Sheila her only friend would listen, say "It'll be alright, Prim" and comfort her but what could she say in these circumstances?

As she passed the first class carriages, she muttered to herself *All bloody empty*. For a while after boarding the train she had had the first standard class carriage to herself, but it was slowly filling up. A pretty young girl got on and, much to Prim's relief, was immediately intent on her iPhone. Every so often Prim sighed deeply. *This is a great time to be without a proper tissue*, she thought. *Life is so full of small things that one forgets*. She knew tears were forming and that her nose would soon start to run. She also knew how she must appear to the other passengers, thoroughly dishevelled and a picture of total despair, but she didn't care. *So what?*

She noticed that the other passengers were being careful to avoid sitting next to her or even making eye contact with her. *Good*, she thought. She could almost hear what they were thinking and felt like confirming their suspicions. "Yes," she wanted to yell. "I'm the nutter on the train. I'm a total loser, I've lost everything."

Prim was not naturally bitter but she was overwhelmed by the unfairness of her situation. Her inner child's voice wanted to shout "It's not fair!" She wanted to shake the other passengers, to make them aware that what had happened to her could happen to them. "Just wait till you come up against the welfare state," she would say. "You might lose everything. It's impossible to beat the system. I failed, so will you. *They* have all the power and we have none. *They* are the experts and we are slow and stupid. I'm sixty but they spoke to me as if I were a small, slow child."

Exhausted by the vigour of her own thoughts she sighed once more. *On the other hand*, she thought, *these people on the train won't listen, and I'm beyond caring what they think of me. They might as well know I had to be escorted out of the building by security and was given a warning.* Prim felt the tension rise and her fists clench at the thought of the security guard. She realised she was gnawing her knuckles. *How dare that pompous arse of a security guard tell me that the* nice social work lady *was actually doing me a favour by talking to me because she wasn't obliged to do so. Well thanks very much!*

Prim spent the time until the train left by resenting the other passengers as they got on, and trying to wear a *Don't sit next to me* expression on her face. At one point, when a woman wearing flip-flops and no coat appeared, Prim wondered whether she might not be the only nutter on the train. *That's downright weird in this weather – she looks really spaced out*, she thought.

Just after the doors closed, the last passenger to get on headed Prim's way and she took an instant dislike to him. He was the perfect target for her silent rant, expensively dressed but appearing nervous, almost as dishevelled as herself and perspiring profusely. He had obviously rushed to catch the train and, as he sat down, he nearly swiped her with his briefcase.

"Be a bit more careful with that, sir. You don't want to cause GBH now do you?" she said, but he either didn't hear her or he decided to ignore her.

*Too important to talk to me*, she thought. *A banker type who's upset that he only got a one million bonus instead of two because of the financial crisis. A crisis which he and his like caused in the first place.*

As the train moved out, Prim's nose started to run and her thoughts ran too. She sniffed loudly. *Mr Banker is giving me dirty looks every time I sniff*, she thought. *Well tough. I'm going to sniff all the way to Peterborough, so too bad for you mate. If you get on last, you have to sit next to the designated carriage nutter. Why is this banker on the train anyway? Maybe his Ferrari's in the garage and his spare's being used by Mrs Banker. And why isn't he in first class? Silly bugger, taking up room here when he doesn't have to. I'm going to let him know what I think of him. I'm going to tell him how the cuts he's caused have affected me and hundreds like me. I'm going to let him have it. He doesn't care about anyone but himself. Oh look, he has the most expensive phone you can buy. Most probably on the company, and why doesn't he turn the bloody thing off? Just wait, soon he'll be saying I'm on the train. Of course he bloody well is. He jumps every time the bloody thing rings and it's disturbing my thoughts.*

Prim continued to rant silently as the train made its way through the north London suburbs. She had done this journey many times to give support to – or to receive it from – Sheila and she was not interested in the scenery, or lack of it, that unfurled past the windows of the train. Instead, she thought she should try to make sense of the day. Getting herself worked up about the annoying banker, with his stupid trade-mark red braces, wouldn't help. She couldn't quite believe the position she found herself in and, what was worse, there was nothing she could do about it. *Surely?* she thought. *Surely if I had*

*explained things better, more accurately, Ms Took would have seen sense*
*and calamity would not have descended on me.* One thing she did
know was that she didn't want to hear the phrase 'in your own
best interest' ever again. The social worker had seemed so kind
as she patiently explained to Prim that it was in her own best
interest for the welfare state to take every penny her family had
ever saved and, when that ran out, to take the home she had
lived in since birth. Ms Took made it seem like a good idea that
the welfare state would make her homeless in the next four to
six months. She could never, in her wildest imaginings, have
believed that it would come to this – but it had.

Prim thought about her failure to communicate with the
social worker. She was not good with words, and when under
pressure she was even more tongue-tied. She tried to explain
that she didn't see how it was in either her own or her aunt's
best interests to lose everything. Ms Took had explained, slowly,
carefully and, to Prim's mind, most patronisingly that they, the
people at the meeting, had a duty of care towards her aunt who,
she pointed out, was not *really* her aunt. "In fact," she said, "you
and Miss Rose are not related at all." She said that Miss Rose was,
in effect, her landlady and she had, all along, been acting as no
more than a part-time carer for her 'aunt', Miss Rose.

Trying to adopt the same tone of voice as Ms Took, Prim
said, "My aunt just wants to go home, and I just want to take
her home and look after her. I am perfectly capable of doing
that. I will give up my job to care for her."

Ms Took intervened, saying, "Miss Rose, because of her
condition, needs 24/7 care. As you and your aunt, I mean Miss
Rose, live on your own, that would mean you could not leave
her unattended. You could not go out, even for a few minutes,
unless someone else was in the house. That person could not
be just *anyone* because Miss Rose needs professional nursing
care. It really would be very difficult for you to cope. You might
hurt yourself lifting her on your own, and there would be very

little respite help for you with the cuts we have to impose. It really is in your own best interest to place your aunt, I mean Miss Rose, in a home where she will have the standard of care she needs and deserves."

"I *can* look after her," Prim stated. "I know her better than anyone else. I love her more than any stranger could. I know what she needs and likes. No one else could care for her the way I do. I don't *need* to go out, I can shop online. We've looked after each other all our lives. She is more than just my *aunt* – she is my whole family." She tried to stop her voice rising and nearly choked with the effort. Ms Took's kindly, understanding expression infuriated Prim and anger took the place of pleading. "You can't stop me taking her home. This is a free country and home is where she wants to live. You can't do this to us. You have no right!"

Ms Took then said the one thing which was certain to exacerbate Prim's anger. She called her by the name she never used. "Miss Russo," she said. "I'm very sorry to have to point out that it is *you* who has no right to make decisions for Miss Rose. You are not her next of kin, you are not even a blood relation, whereas we have the responsibility and legal obligation to act in Miss Rose's best interest."

Prim's fist landed on the desk inches away from Ms Took's coffee cup, spilling the hot liquid all over her. The two women both jumped up at the same time. Prim shouted, "Don't call me that. My name is not Russo. My name is Rose. I have always been Primavera Rose."

The motion of the train rocked Prim in a soothing, consoling manner as she remembered the pride she felt in her strong words. She allowed herself a small smile at the thought of covering Ms Took with hot coffee. It felt like a small victory, but it was a victory which meant that security was called for the first time that day.

Prim felt a bit guilty as Ms Took left the room to change her suit. It looked new, and was in stark contrast to the track suit the social worker was wearing when she returned. This time she was accompanied by two security guards and had clearly spent a few minutes gathering her composure. It showed in her voice when she spoke.

"I feel huge sympathy for your plight. I know the implications of this meeting for you and I am simply doing my job, delivering a difficult message. Let's be honest about this: you won't be able to raise a mortgage to keep your aunt's – Miss Rose's – home as you are too old. It's a great shame that you and Miss Rose did not make yourselves tenants in common. You have very little chance of getting a housing association home as you are too far down the list and, as a single employed person, you are a low priority. With the pressure on the private rented sector, you will be lucky if you could even find somewhere to rent. But you need to understand that yours is far from the worst case I have seen. The cuts are hitting hard and there are children hours away from being on the streets. I know it doesn't seem fair, but you must remember that the social services department does not have a bottomless pit of money to spend. And, after all, Miss Rose will be well cared for and you are an adult of sound mind and body and you are gainfully employed as a cook in a school. You are in a far better position than most of my clients."

*Thanks very much*, Prim thought as she sat and listened to this, red-faced and smouldering with frustration. Although she refused to calm down, she was grateful when Ms Took announced that she would try to finish the meeting – Prim did not want her to postpone it and have to go through this all over again. She even stammered an apology, saying that she was sorry for causing such an unfortunate accident and offering to pay for the clothes to be cleaned. Ms Took accepted the apology and asked the pair from security to leave.

Ms Took then apologised. "I'm sorry if calling you Miss Russo upset you, but it is the name on your birth certificate."

Prim explained that her mother and father put that name on the birth certificate because it was the right thing to do; it was the truth, and her mother always told the truth. "But he isn't the father I knew," she said. "He didn't bring me up."

Prim was jolted back to the present by the train coming to a sudden stop. Mr Banker was nearly thrown out of his seat. *Good*, she thought.

An announcement brought her thoughts to a complete halt.

**We apologise for the delay. A train ahead of us has broken down. We will keep you informed, but expect to continue our journey shortly.**

*Typical*, she thought, before arrogant Mr Banker asked her a really stupid question.

"Where are we?"

Prim resisted saying *On the bloody 15:08 from King's Cross to York*, and just snapped, "I haven't a clue."

*Stupid bugger keeps interrupting.* The interruption was almost welcome because she was remembering, with some pain, her total failure to explain to Ms Took the close and loving relationship she had enjoyed with her father and her aunt. She wanted the people at the meeting to know what sort of family they had been, what sort of people they were.

She told them, instead, that she had recently applied to become a prison visitor. When her best friend Sheila's father was sent to prison for fraud in the 1960s, Prim had supported her even though they were quite young teenagers at the time. Sheila was too scared to visit her father on her own and Prim was the only friend who would go with her. When the rest of the street spurned what remained of the family, Prim and Auntie Rose still invited Sheila and her mother to tea. Although the neighbours still did not speak to *that family*, they all had a lurid interest in what it was like to visit a real prison and Prim

140

discovered that she had gained kudos. "What's it like?" they would ask. "Will you meet any murderers?" She enjoyed the attention and, even before she'd started the training course, had begun to think of herself as an expert. As part of the assessment programme, she had visited an open prison and found it really interesting.

As Prim talked, she could see that Ms Took was not interested. She clearly thought it was irrelevant and didn't want to know what the family was like: she just wanted to get on with the meeting. Prim had a thought and fished in her bag for an old newspaper clipping: *This will do it.* She started to read the article to Ms Took. Prim's hope was that she would see that her family did not deserve to be treated like this. They had done their bit for Queen and Country.

> *The Sunday Times* – Obituary August 2004
> Fifty years ago 600 soldiers of the British Army took on a force of 30,000 Chinese troops crossing the Imjin River in Korea.
>
> Reporting to his American superior, Brigadier Thomas Brodie of the Gloucestershire Regiment admitted the situation was 'a bit sticky'.
>
> Such classic British understatement failed to secure the 'Glorious Glosters' reinforcements or permission to fall back.
>
> At the end of the battle 10,000 Chinese troops had fallen. British losses stood at just fifty-nine, but only thirty-nine of the survivors evaded capture.
>
> Several Victoria Crosses, Britain's highest military honour, were awarded for the action. One was given to Captain Augustus Rose, who died this month after a long illness.
>
> Despite such heroism, Britain's role in the conflict has largely been forgotten by the public . . .

At this point Ms Took interrupted Prim. "Thank you for bringing this to the meeting but . . . "

Prim held up her hand, stopping Ms Took in her tracks. "That man was my father. He was the only father I ever knew, a hero. He won the Victoria Cross and he and my aunt brought me up."

Ms Took tried to regain control of the meeting but she did not now know what to call Prim. She did not want a repeat of the situation when she called her 'Miss Russo'. So she started to call her 'Miss Umh'. "Let's take a short break," she said.

Prim's reverie was broken, once again. *Why doesn't that bloody phone of his stop ringing?* She cursed silently, staring at Mr Banker. She noticed that the train was still stationary, but she didn't care: *I have to think about what Ms Took said.*

Prim remembered having a cigarette outside during that short break before Ms Took resumed the meeting. It then went from bad to worse: "Miss . . . Umh. As you know, this is your final appeal. We have looked into the case very carefully and it is our understanding that you are not related to Miss Rose. We understand that your mother, Miss Else Wood, was engaged to Mr Augustus Rose when he was serving in Korea. We further understand that when Mr Rose came back from Korea, badly injured, the engagement was broken off but Mr Rose and Miss Wood remained close friends. Miss Wood moved into the Roses' family home and helped Miss Rose, Mr Augustus Rose's sister, to look after him and to try nursing him back to health. You were born after Miss Wood had a brief relationship with a Mr Salvatore Russo. We also understand that, sadly, your mother died when you were just eighteen months old and that your father, Mr Russo, could not be traced."

*Could not be traced – that's putting it mildly*, Prim thought. "Yes," she said. "He named me then scarpered back to his wife in Italy, never to be seen again, when she found out about me. So he is not my father, he had no part in my upbringing."

Ms Took replied "We understand that your biological father was not around at that time and you were taken in by Mr Rose and his sister."

"Taken in? Taken in like a lost puppy!" Prim cried. "They did more than just *take me in* – they loved and cared for me. They told me I was a gift, the best gift my mother could have left them."

"Yes, I understand that," said Ms Took. "But unfortunately they did not formally adopt you."

"They couldn't," Prim roared, even louder than before. "In those days single men and women were not allowed to adopt. My father was a war hero and it didn't even count that they were brother and sister living together perfectly respectably. They were single and the stupid rules at the time did not allow it. If you ask me it was plain bloody criminal."

Ms Took continued, with some difficulty. "But they did not inform the authorities of the informal arrangement."

"Of course not," said Prim. "And a good job too. They kept me out of sight of your lot because, if you had known about me, I would have been fostered out to strangers or sent off to a children's home to be abused or sent off to Australia to be a farm slave!"

Prim's fist came down again and security was called for the second time. She apologised almost immediately and the call for security was cancelled.

Ms Took went on to explain that she was *acting in Miss Rose's best interest*. Miss Rose needed twenty-four-hour professional nursing care, she explained, so it was also in Miss Uhm's best interest to place Miss Rose in a home. She said that, very soon, because of the worsening state of Miss Rose's dementia she would no longer recognise Miss Umh. She said that her office could let Miss Uhm have a list of nearby homes. Ms Took said she was not allowed to recommend a home but she could refer Miss Uhm to the Care Quality Commission. All this went over

Prim's head as she felt herself being overwhelmed with despair. "Now," said Ms Took. "It looks like you are here in the capacity of Miss Rose's representative. That person can be a family member, a legal representative or a friend. We have established that you and Miss Rose are not next of kin, by blood or adoption. You are not dependent on Miss Rose as you have a part-time job and you could return to full-time work, if you wished. You are not tenants in common and you are not married or in a civil partnership."

Prim heard herself exclaim, "You mean if I had married my aunt we would not be in this situation! How weird is that?"

Ms Took ploughed on. "We will now go through the Decision Support Tool document. As you know, the DST is used to assess the needs of the patient and to assess whether they qualify for funding, depending on how they score in each of the twelve domains. We will go through it so that you understand the reasons for our decisions."

Prim knew she had lost. They had not listened to a word she'd said. They did not care how close she and her aunt were. That did not matter. All that mattered was how many points her aunt scored on this nonsensical document. They weren't in the least interested in her aunt as a whole human being who'd once had a life.

Prim had been sent a copy of the hated document. She had read it, but she did not really understand it. She could not believe that anyone with an ounce of common sense would take the parts she *did* understand at all seriously. It looked like something Al Capone would call a *legitimate racket*. Its sole purpose was to extract money from the vulnerable so that the so-called welfare state did not have to find the cash to support them. If it all went badly, she planned to use the mountain of paperwork to set fire to her home – she might as well take drastic action as the house was no longer hers. She had done some research and she thought this document was the most evil thing ever invented to help the NHS, Social Services and the Treasury wriggle out of their 1948 promise to look after the country's citizens from the cradle to the grave.

She heard another announcement.

**We regret to inform you that we will be unable to move on for up to an hour. Engineers are working as fast as possible to clear the other train from the line. Meanwhile, we ask for your patience. The buffet car is open.**

Bloody great, Prim thought. I hate trains; they always do this to me. But when I'm homeless I might be one of those people riding the underground all day just to keep warm, so I'd better get used to them.

Prim found herself staring at a distant church spire. Her aunt had been a regular church-goer. That generation had believed in the post-war welfare state and were proud of it. They understood that, if you were honest and you worked hard, fought for your country and paid your taxes, in return you would be looked after in your old age. How wrong they were.

Like many people of their age, Prim's father and aunt had struggled to buy their modest home. They thought they were lucky because they had some savings in the bank which they hoped to leave to her. They had no idea that if you got old and ill you could lose the lot to some care home fat cat, like that banker opposite.

*He might be one of them. I'll bet he employs people on slave labour rates and that he bullies, beats and insults the residents,* she thought, before her mind turned back to the reality of her situation. *When is this train going to start?* She rested her head against the window, not caring how dirty it was. She thought about Ms Took going through the hated document, and felt her anger rise again. One of the domains or categories was mobility. Prim had been absolutely certain that her aunt would qualify under

145

this heading because she simply could not move. She had not walked since she had broken a hip in her last fall and now her muscles were wasted to nothing. Despite the best efforts of the physiotherapist to get her to stand, Miss Rose had determinedly stayed put. It hurt her too much and she had had enough. Prim had heard her aunt address language she had not realised she knew to the physiotherapist. *Bugger off, you stupid cow* was not a phrase much heard in the Rose household.

This sort of language was so out of character for her aunt that Prim had become really upset. It was made worse by a casual remark from a nurse who said, "Well, yes. Patients with dementia can get like that." This was the first time Prim had heard the word *dementia* in relation to her aunt. She was shocked by its brutal finality and by the uncaring and casual way she had found out about her aunt's condition.

Prim looked at her watch: the train must have been immobile for at least an hour. There had been other announcements which she had not bothered to listen to while she let her thoughts drift, remembering her aunt. Auntie Rose had been her rock, sheltering Prim and bringing her up in the 1950s style which meant you did not question authority. Policemen, doctors and social workers were respected and obeyed. They knew what was best for you. Now Prim was struggling against her upbringing and her nature in order to question and disagree with everything the articulate Ms Took was saying. It was only anger and bitterness that kept her going. She had never felt she was a match for clever people. She knew her own education had not been up to much and she had been bullied and taunted at school because she was illegitimate: they called her a *bastard*. This behaviour stopped when her father started picking her up from school wearing his Victoria Cross. The other parents would shake his hand and give their offspring a clip round the ear for being cheeky. Prim remembered her aunt saying, "Everything will be alright, Primmy. You are our little ray of sunshine. Your mummy left us the best gift she ever could in you and don't let anyone tell you different. We all love you and this is your home for ever."

Now the home she had always lived in was going to be taken away and Prim would be homeless and alone. She felt keenly that if only she could have explained things better, if she could have been more articulate like Ms Took, they would have understood.

Prim sniffed again, uncontrollably and louder than before. This earned her a special glare from the banker, and she glared back. *He and his type were the ones who created the Decision Support Tool,* she thought. *Why doesn't he switch his bloody phone off? I can't think straight with him fiddling and talking all the time. I need to clear my mind so I can think about what I must do. It's no good dwelling on the past. Why hasn't the bloody train started? Typical rail service these days. Mr Banker there is in a cold sweat. He'll be missing his multi-million pound deal and won't be able to buy his fourth Ferrari. What a shame.*

She wanted to hit someone, and the banker was nearest. *Look at him,* she thought. *All nervy twitches, jumping every time his bloody state-of-the-art mobile rings. 'Oh! I'm so important. So many people need to talk to important, successful me. Oh and my wife can't wait for me to rush home with pots of money so she can buy another handbag.' That bag would be worth double my measly monthly salary as a part-time cook.*

Prim thought again about the meeting, about how she had begged to be allowed to look after her aunt. She had already gone from full-time work to part-time so she could care for her aunt, and it hadn't been easy. She knew that she snapped at her aunt sometimes and had occasionally been unkind. She felt very guilty a lot of the time but she really had tried her best. She told Ms Took, "I'll give up my job to care for my aunt full-time."

"But," Ms Took said, "Your aunt must have qualified nursing care."

147

For a fraction of a moment, Prim thought she had spotted a chink in the armour of their case and she gave voice to what sounded like a logical argument. "If she needs qualified nursing care, why doesn't she qualify to be nursed by the NHS? Everyone else who is sick does."

"Ah," said Ms Took, trying hard to look like a kindly benefactor. "The NHS *will* cover her nursing costs." Prim felt joyful relief for a second or two before she was told that that would amount to little more than £100 a week. She knew that a nursing home would cost at least £700 a week so, even after her aunt's pension had been handed over, she would have to find the balance. *Full-time pay is not bad for a cook, but I still couldn't afford that*, she thought.

The smile on Ms Took's face as she explained that Miss Rose would get at least £109 a week for nursing care was too much for Prim. Her fist came down for the last time. She knocked a jug of water into Ms Took's lap and this time the social worker reacted furiously. Security was called, and Prim was escorted from the building.

Being marched out was mortifying and the embarrassment she felt gave Prim an insight into how the inmates of the open prison might feel when they were arrested. Most of them appeared to be OK. She'd really liked listening to their stories and she knew prison visiting would give her the chance to meet people she would not normally come across in her daily life. She thought some of them had been driven to crime by circumstances, and she could relate to that. She thought she would like to specialise in helping new inmates adjust to life in the open prison. She sniffed loudly again, not caring about those around her, and to her surprise the evil banker held out a tissue.

"Thank you. I'm sorry about the sniffing," she said. "It's been a really bad day."

"Tell me about it," he said. Prim was going to, but his phone lit up and pinged and he took another call.

The train had still not moved. It must have been well over an hour now. Prim noticed that a few of the other passengers were chatting. Some of them looked really fed up and the banker was clearly very uncomfortable and troubled. Perhaps he needed the loo but several of the loos were out of order, no doubt overflowing, so he had better forget it.

Mustn't think ill of the banker. After all, he did give me a tissue but I'm sure he can afford that.

Tired of thinking about her own troubles, Prim started to eavesdrop on the banker's calls. It was the only entertainment she had. He seemed to be talking about a crime someone had committed, saying, "Sounds dodgy to me. Some people might even call it fraud, although this anonymous trader would probably have covered his tracks at least well enough to keep the auditors off the scent. Listen, Dennis, I'm on a train *en route* to a business meeting . . . I can't discuss it now. Let's talk about it over a beer at lunch tomorrow." He hung up.

"You're talking about fraud?" asked Prim. "That's very interesting."

"What?" spluttered the banker.

Blimey! He looks as if he's seen a ghost, thought Prim.

She repeated the question. "I said *fraud*. Are you talking about committing fraud?"

"No, you've got the wrong end of the stick. We were talking about a TV programme, on last night – some bloke at a Japanese bank." Prim could spot an obvious lie and she decided to have a bit of fun with the banker.

"No, *you've* got the wrong end of the stick. I'm interested because I need to commit one, not because of what you or your pals may have done. It's just you look the kind of bloke who understands this sort of thing and could give me some tips."

Mr Banker spluttered something else about TV then held up his *Financial Times* and Prim found herself talking to the

149

back of his newspaper. *He didn't get the joke,* she thought, before she continued speaking.

"I'm only interested because I know about prisons. I've read quite a lot and I'm going to be a prison visitor. Most of the guys who do fraud eventually end up in a nice open prison. If your friend gets sent down, tell him it's not so bad. He'll do some hard time at first but then, if he keeps his nose clean, he'll be sent to an open prison. It's nothing to be frightened of. They don't put the real hard nuts in there. I already know that the prisoners cook the food themselves so I'm going to give them cooking tips. Some prisoners even go home for the weekends. There's a library, you've got books, telly and anything really. You can do any type of gym and an Open University course. There are clubs and rehabilitation. Lots of nice prison visitors too and . . ."

The *FT* stayed firmly in place so Prim stopped talking. *OK! Sod you,* she thought. *Maybe he is an evil shit after all.* She sat looking out of the window. *Screw him.* She was only trying to help him and his friend. Helping was in her nature. She was normally the person who would say "Don't worry! It might never happen." That might not go down well on prison visits but she hoped some of the inmates would smile.

The train still hadn't moved but Prim didn't care. The delay gave her time to think. After this visit to Sheila, she only had the lonely house to go back to. She loved the home she had known since childhood but, without her father and her aunt, it was just full of the most painful and poignant memories.

With no other entertainment she considered the banker again. *Yeah. He's committed a fraud,* she thought. *I can spot them.* From her prison visitor induction course and from the detective novels and TV shows she loved watching, Prim considered herself very knowledgeable but, as someone once said, "A little knowledge is a dangerous thing" and she often got the wrong end of the stick. *He won't get away with it. I may soon be visiting you, mate,* she thought.

A small germ of an idea started to form in Prim's mind. She was certain she was going to lose her home to pay for her aunt's care. What she had told Mr I'm-so-important Banker was true. The open prison she had visited wasn't a bad place. She had met a lot of the inmates: some of them were really very nice and others she recognised from the stories that had been in the newspapers. There was the toff who had tried to commit insurance fraud by setting light to his vintage Rolls Royce. He had a conscience and owned up before the insurers coughed up but he still got two years. There was the MP who was very economical with the truth over his expenses and who was shopped by his wife when she found out about his mistress. There was Adrian, quite the *artiste*: some of his forgeries were still displayed in galleries and he was also very good at copying documents. Miles described himself as *a bit naughty* when he forged his dead wife's signature on a will and tried to disinherit his horrible step-children. There were also quite a few financial advisors who had embezzled thousands from their clients. Patrick had got almost two million from his horrible teenage rock star client and most of it was still stashed somewhere.

You really have to be quite clever to pull this stuff off, thought Prim. I would most probably not be clever enough. The germ then blossomed into a fully formed idea. I might not want to get away with it. It really is OK in there.

She thought about the inmates and how they all got on very well. Prim thought she could even help them with ideas of how to make birthday cakes for each other. She had heard that they would share cigarettes, magazines and books and look out for each other.

No wonder some of them didn't want to leave. For the first time in their lives they didn't have to worry about being caught. They could be themselves. There was a free exchange of ideas like, for example, how to improve your accounting methods. Often inmates left with a much better idea of how to manage their affairs.

"This is the best university I've ever been in," one professor was reported as saying as he left. He had been sentenced for selling exam papers to wealthy overseas students. His profitable sideline had gone on for many years until age made him get the exams mixed up and he sold last year's papers for this year's exams. He might have got away with it but he had to own up when some Chinese syndicate boss's son failed the exam. Prison was the safest place for him.

Another announcement annoyed Prim.

> **We apologise for the delay. The broken train has just been moved out of Huntingdon station. Due to the length of time we have been stationary, we will be making a short, unscheduled stop at Huntingdon. Any passengers wishing to alight there should prepare to do so.**

Prim thought, *Oh shut up with the bloody announcements. I was thinking. Now then, what was I thinking? Safe, that's it. Prison is safe. A home with no rent. Great! That's how I solve my housing problem! Right then, you bastards. A life of crime it is.* She would get caught, do a bit of hard time and then she'd be sent to a lovely open prison. The more she thought about it, the more appealing it seemed.

At last the train was moving again and even banker man seemed to have calmed down. Thinking of her new life in prison Prim could only see the benefits. No one would miss her. She would have a roof over her head. It was warm in winter with no heating bills. She could even go out for weekends and visit her aunt. She could have her own telly so she could watch her favourite soaps all day long. She would be the best cook they ever had and she could even try to improve her education, do an OU course in criminology or something like that. If the welfare state was not going to look after her aunt then it would

152

have to look after her instead, and at considerably greater expense. *That'll teach them!*

Prim had to decide which crime to commit to get into an open prison. She had tried to talk to the prison officers about who did what, but they were too professional to let on. Sheila had given her a bit of information, but not much. Prim had found out that for a first offence you often got a fine and that they didn't really like sending women to prison, so she would have to build up a good criminal CV.

*Snails could go faster than this train,* she thought. Then it hit her. *Train fraud.* She laughed out loud. She could tear up her ticket now and pretend she had never bought it. She could confess but show no remorse. That would be a brilliant start. She would admit to a long history of train fraud, like that man in the papers. She could say that she had not paid for a ticket since the early 1980s. She could say she didn't care because she was working against capitalism and the train companies deserved it. The trains were always late, even cancelled, without regard for the huddled masses in the stations. Last Christmas was a nightmare. She could say if the bankers can get away with massive fraud, then why not her?

What a brilliant plan! When this train arrives at Huntingdon I'll go straight to the ticket office and tell them how glad I am that I hadn't paid for a ticket because the service was terrible. But the length of this delay meant they would probably try to compensate all the passengers and they'd know she had bought a ticket. She thought of pulling the communication cord and stopping the train. That might cause Mr Banker opposite to wet himself as he seemed to be panicking again.

*Yes. I might pull the cord,* she thought. *I'm going to get back at the system. I'm going to do it now!*

But as she looked at the anxious faces around her she knew she could not pull the cord. There might be people on the train who would suffer if the delay was even longer. Even though she was very bitter at the moment, generally she was not so bad and had a soft side. She didn't really want to hurt anyone.

Committing a crime without upsetting anyone will be much more difficult than I thought, she mused. But I have a head start. I have real experts to advise me. I'll take notes next time I visit the prison.

She glanced at Mr Banker again. He looked like his head was about to explode. *I don't mind hurting him though, not one bit,* she thought. *I'll just have a bit more fun with him. I'll let him know I know he's a banker.* She tried to start a conversation. "You seem to have a lot of worries." He wasn't interested in talking so she turned back to her thoughts. *But thank you, Mr Banker, for giving me the fraud idea and starting my new career as the most unsuccessful criminal ever. Good job the train was delayed. It gave me time to think.*

**This is Huntingdon. Will passengers leaving the train here please make sure they have all their baggage with them.**

Maybe I could steal the banker's baggage, that briefcase he keeps looking at, Prim thought as some of the passengers prepared to get off the train. If he gets off, I'll follow him out of the station. He won't notice me, no one ever does, but then I'll sneak up, grab it and do a runner. That's a great start! She closed her eyes and sat back, thinking about how great this idea was and planning how she could make sure she was caught red-handed. Prim got so wrapped up in her daydream that, before she could put her plan into action, the train pulled out of Huntingdon station. By then, Mr Banker and his case had already made their getaway. She gave a private, knowing smirk. *Next time,* she thought.

# Just in case
by Richard Hopgood

H I there, how you doing? I'm Andy. Thirty-five. City trader in an investment bank. Well, you can probably tell that from the braces. Don't always wear them, but I was definitely wearing them that day.

I have this theory, you know, that when stuff starts to go wrong, it carries on going wrong. If I believed in the supernatural, I'd say somebody had the evil eye on me. That's what my wife would say – and she'd start mumbling one of those prayers which she knows irk me no end. I don't believe in it so it's either chance or some obscure law of physics, a kind of hidden gravity of events.

Anyway, enough trying to fathom the unfathomable.

It started with a phone call. I was in the office after lunch, packing my briefcase with papers I wouldn't look at and trying to pick a moment when the boss was on the phone. Otherwise he would call me in to tell me how brilliant he is and what a shame it is I'm not more like him. Banter, he calls it. Bollocks, more like it. Anyway, I clocked he was on another phone call and was about to slide out when my own phone rang. Private number, undisclosed.

"Don't be late," a voice said at the other end.

"Is that you, Micky?" I asked.

"Just don't be late," he said, and hung up.

Well, it had to be him but it might not have been, if you know what I mean. I'm a cautious bloke, so I logged into my calendar in case there was something I'd forgotten about, a drink with another trader or somebody's birthday bash at the Wellington Arms. Nothing. *Hmm*, I thought. *If he'd just said* Yes *I wouldn't have had to go through all this rigmarole and waste a couple of minutes*. Needless to say the boss was off the phone by the time I went past his office door.

"Hold your horses," he shouted after me. I turned and stood in his doorway.

"I'm late," I said. "In a rush."

"I just need to check out a few things."

It's fatal to hesitate, but I did. I was thinking *What bleeding things?* as if he might really, for the first time ever, have something serious to check out. We all do stuff which is a bit over the line and he knows we do it, even though he doesn't know what. Anyway it was nothing, just a ruse for him to boast of his latest triumphs, to gossip about his own boss whom he pretends to like but actually loathes. I expect you're thinking that where I work doesn't sound very nice. You wouldn't be wrong, but the money is very nice indeed.

As I was buttoning my coat and standing up he looked at me with a funny expression, sort of weighing me up. "Next week, Andy," he said, "we've got a special audit." They're sending in the jobsworths to scrutinise every trade over one million pounds during the last few months. A special request from the Chairman."

"Good," I said, letting a mask of impassivity settle over my face. "About time too. Some of the guys are getting a bit gung ho."

"Gung ho? *Gung ho?*" he grunted. "I should bloody well hope so. We're traders, not bloody bankers!"

He laughed so much he started wheezing then coughing, asthmatically. *Some kind of private joke*, I thought, *unless he suspects, of course*. He's good at that. You never know quite what he's thinking. But then he might say the same about me. He winks as I leave.

It's already two-thirty. I leg it to the tube station. A few tourists are meandering across my line of vision, staring up at the big new buildings and cranes as if they have never seen anything so high before. One of them takes out the inevitable camera and tries to organise his mates into an impromptu group photo, kneeling down so he can shoot their heads against the skyline. I walk across his camera line as he clicks and he looks at me, quizzically. *Some of us have got jobs to do*, I mouth. The rest of us are walking fast; if we were horses it would be a brisk trot, not running but not walking either. We're all at it, in a semi-controlled kind of rush. Only my rush is worse than usual.

I go down to the tube station and look at the board. *Minor Delays*. Great. I hop back up the stairs and hail a cab. "King's Cross, mate, quick as you can." The driver shrugs, heads towards the nearest queue of traffic, thinks better of it and turns up a narrow side street, rattling along past startled shoppers and doormen. I rifle a tenner from my wallet, have a quick look at the mobile and sigh. *Why am I always in such a fucking rush?* I lean back in the seat, take a deep breath, and watch the buildings drift by as we make our way through a maze of back roads and side streets, then up the Gray's Inn Road. Things quieten down; we're out of the City now, the shops get shabbier and the walkers amble, aimlessly, as if they're killing time.

King's Cross. Dash from the taxi, find a machine, buy a ticket, glancing out of the corner of my eye all the time at the departures board, at the flickering appearance and disappearance of destinations and stations, departure times and platforms. I can't stop it; I'm scanning the display like a computer screen of prices, only this is all white, no colour coding of blues and reds to signify the price changes up and down. All the while announcements are booming, instructions not to leave luggage unattended and the background noise of jazz and rock playing in cafés and shops. People pause, wait, surge forward, linger, move their heads up and down and to the side, just like the pigeons pottering around pecking at paper and crumbs, tossing them in the air, then peering right and left to look for the latest careless manna from above.

Well, I'm on the train now. Not my normal one – and not my normal time. And not the train I wanted to catch, thanks to the boss. Mid-afternoon, a few other City boys bunking off early, mums with kids, students with rucksacks, a few business types who are immediately on their phone or laptop tapping away in their own little bubbles of work. A few shabby types who look like they're just here for the ride, with their little notebooks and biros and furtive observations. Spies probably, shuttling up and down the East Coast line on the lookout for suspicious types and faces. Well, don't look at me Charlie boy, I'm a respectable man on respectable business. Aren't I . . . ?

I grab the first seat I see, next to a dumpy woman who seems to be crying, soundlessly, and drying her eyes on a serviette. Well, it takes all sorts. Another time I might ask her what's wrong, but this is *this* time and I've got a lot on my mind. As I sit down I look at her sensible brown shoes, beneath the table and her thick brown tights, the kind of thing my mother used to wear before she stopped being practical. Her feet are saying *Don't desire me, or even like me – or I might kick you*. Her expression, when she glances at me, is not much different. I can see we're going to get on like a house on fire.

I put my case up on the rack. Just an ordinary case. I know what you're thinking: *What you got in there Andy?* A few papers, if you must know; *Sporting Life*, *City A.M.*, the *Metro* – I'm not highbrow. Oh yes, and fifty thousand quid. In used notes. Twenty bundles of £2,500 each – mainly in £20 notes. I would have preferred £50s, but they are more easily traced. Now to you £50,000 is probably a bloody fortune. For me, it isn't. Not

159

enough noughts on the end for that. We trade in millions. But this is cash. Real cash, and that's something different.

I can see you licking your lips and wondering how you can get your hands on it. Well calm down, dear reader, your hands ain't going nowhere. If you like, I'll take a bundle down later just so you can sniff it. The smell of used money – paper and ink and human sweat with an occasional tincture of cocaine and alcohol. A heady mixture, my good friend. I've borrowed it from Billy, my bookie. I'm way over my credit limit with him but he knows my luck will turn. And with the profit I make on this he can make his money back, what I owe him and quite a bit on top. He trusts me. It's going to be alright. Money always makes money, the first law of trading; that's what I told him. I've done it before for Billy, trading on my own account for him, but this is different. A bit off-piste. Sort of.

I'm on my way to see Micky. Lithe little bloke with a black quiff and darting eyes and a sharp line in Italian shoes. An Essex boy, like me. He sold me a car once, an Alfa Romeo Spider. Very beautiful, with an engine noise like an aria, great when she was on song but very temperamental and always thirsty. Anyway, Micky and me became mates. He'd do me a few favours when it was time to change the motor. I steered a few of my City pals his way. We'd go and watch West Ham when they were home to Arsenal or Spurs. He was doing well, and I was doing well. Then he got married and moved up to the Midlands. Started selling new cars as well as second-hand with a big showroom. Told me he was going to make a fortune. Only it didn't happen. The new cars wouldn't shift and he started to owe too much money. Micky's not a quitter so he found some new ways to make money, on the side. Allowed some blokes to keep hot cars in his lock-ups before they moved them on. Arranged some resprays and new plates. All just oiling the wheels so to speak, nothing too heavy. He didn't tell me about it to begin with, but he gradually let on. I'd ask him about the new Merc he was driving and since when had he started buying silk shirts, and he'd smirk and say it was good for business. *People like to see you thriving*, he said. *They think you must be good at your job.* Well, I could understand that. In my world, you need to show a bit just to prove you're making a bit.

Anyway, to cut to the chase, Micky's got some big deal on, cash only, treble your money, no questions asked. So I'm going to deliver the cash. In some poxy little town in Nottinghamshire. I'm the banker. Exactly what the deal is, well you don't need to know. All that matters is that a week today I'll make the same trip and come back with two suitcases rather than one. Micky will be happy. I'll be back in credit and ready to flutter. Billy will be over the moon, big time. And we'll all get back to our everyday business. Shocked? Well, don't be. We're the entrepreneurs, the wealth creators . . .

We're rolling out of London now. The houses get meaner then bigger as we glide through the outer suburbs. There's parks and golf courses, and big back gardens with daffodils and cherry blossom. My kind of manor. I keep glancing up at my case, wondering whether I should put it on my knees to keep it safe. Then the phone vibrates. It's Sharon.

"Where are you?"

"I'm on a train heading north, Petal. Business."

"You're still on for this evening? I've booked a room. It's our anniversary . . . "

"I haven't forgotten," I lie.

"I've bought you something special," she purrs.

"Perfect," I mutter. "Talk later. Love you loads."

I end the call. She's phoning from work – a hairdresser's in Ludgate Circus – so there's no time to chat. We meet every Wednesday after work, for dinner and afters. She's a lovely girl, blonde, long legs, a smart dresser and ambitious. She wants her own salon in Cheam. I'm her business advisor, so to speak. She's got it all worked out. A lot of celebs in Cheam, she says, who all go up the West End to get their barnets styled at £300 a go. Think how much they'd save at £150 a go in her ritzy little salon. You can't argue with the arithmetic, I tell her. Start small, think big. It always puts her in a good mood, dreaming of the fame to come when she's had a hard day in town. Her regular boyfriend, Jake, isn't so keen on the idea but then he wouldn't be. He's an accountant. From Dorking. He doesn't suspect. We're very careful.

The phone beeps again. "Hello, Mum," I say, wondering what she wants this time.

"I'm dying," she whines. "I need you to come and see me."

"What's wrong?" I ask. "Have you taken your tablets?"

"Course I bloody have," she says. "But they don't do me any good any more. I don't see anybody any more. The carers haven't been for weeks."

I heave a heavy sigh. It's not true about the carers, they come three times a day. I should know, they bill me every week, but it's hard to know whether Mum has forgotten or if she's hamming it up. She always liked a bit of melodrama. "What you eating, then?" I ask, wondering whether I can catch her out.

"I'm starving," she croons. "I haven't eaten for days. There's only cat food in the fridge, and I ain't going to let Jimmy starve . . . " Jimmy is a giant ginger cat who could starve for a month and still look fat.

"What about the freezer?"

"I can't touch that, son. You never know when we might have shortages. And you never know when you might have guests."

"No, indeed, Mum."

I explain I'm on a train, a long way away, but I'll be over at the weekend. That seems to satisfy her and she starts telling me about Marty, the budgie, who has learned to greet the milkman every morning with a raucous *Give us a drink!* I tell her I've got to go and she says what a good son I've been. That always gets to me because I haven't got everything right. It probably wasn't a great idea to buy her a bungalow in Bexhill, away from all her friends on the estate, after Dad died. In the summer she's forever complaining about the kids who throw their balls into her front garden by the shingle. And in winter, she moans the place is dead and deserted. She's a gregarious old soul and bustles along to a drop-in parlour once a week but, as she always says every time I see her, *It just ain't the same*. No, it probably ain't.

I start thinking about what I should buy Sharon and, more to the point, how I'm going to find time to buy it before I come back to town. Perhaps Micky will know somewhere in Retford that sells classy gear. Or I can shop in the station when I get back to town. Brown Shoes, opposite me, seems to have stopped snivelling but is now sniffing non-stop. Very unladylike. When you cry you sniff, I muse, so why is she sniffing when she's stopped crying? Or is it simply a cold? You'd think somebody who wears big brown shoes would be sensible enough to have a box of tissues in her big ugly bag.

The phone beeps again. It's a text from Micky. What time you arriving? The guys very particular about the arrangement very jumpy so DONT BE LATE. No idea who this very particular guy is. Micky seems more edgy than usual. He never normally uses capital letters. Don't blame him. £50k is big league by his standards. Anyway, how can I be late? I'm on a train, zooming along at 125 miles an hour, rather than chugging round the M25 and getting nervous every time the brake lights come on ahead. Take the train and avoid the strain. I love a half-empty train; four seats to yourself, gliding through the day and into the night with that rhythmic subdued roar that makes you feel slightly dozy all the time. But this train is heaving, which is a strain in itself, even before you factor in the sniffing.

We stop at Stevenage. Only half an hour to go. I look at my case on the rack, as it nestles there blandly among all the coats and bags of my fellow passengers. Nobody gets up to leave and nobody gets on. So far so good, Micky can relax. Nothing is going to go wrong.

I start thinking about cash. There's something about bundles of notes which makes you feel loaded. Like it's really yours and nobody else's. You can understand these old misers sewing their fortunes into mattresses and stuffing it in secret safes in the wall just so, every once in a while, they can get it out and count it. I think of golden guineas and those big old bank notes. Money was really physical then. I suppose it still is, but where I work you never see it. It's words and numbers. You do a deal, punch in the figures, and money flickers along wires or through the ether, lands in a bank and takes off again, like a ghostly flight of bees searching for a hive. All auditable and traceable, if it's legit, but it's just digits, not money. Carrying all this cash feels like another age, a black and white film, when people queued up at the end of the week to collect their pay packet from the firm's cashier. Happy days . . .

We rumble out of Stevenage, gathering speed. I really should be relaxing, but I can't. Micky's anxiety is contagious. I feel the same as I do when I place a big bet, half-euphoric, half-petrified. Sometimes I can't even bring myself to watch the race so I go for a walk round the block, avoiding the cracks in the pavement for good luck.

The woman opposite glares at me. She seems fixated on my red braces and the silk handkerchief in my top pocket. Then she sniffs so hard it sounds like a snore. I can't bear this and seize a handful of tissues from my pocket and hand them to her. She mutters her thanks and blows her nose, long and hard, before examining the contents of the tissue. I do that myself, but never in public. Not nice. Not nice at all. She seems to notice my irritation and reverts to red-eyed sullenness. I look at her face briefly and think she could look almost pretty with a makeover. Mind you the shoes would have to go, and the coat.

The train slowed down then came to a sudden, jarring stop. I somehow managed to grasp the table with both hands to stop my midriff colliding with its edge. Others were not so lucky and, in the hubbub of alarm, there were a few curses. Then, momentarily, people fell silent, wondering what had happened and waiting for the driver to issue a public explanation. But he didn't. We heard the air hissing out of the brakes. We were in the middle of the countryside, marooned alongside fields and observed by some cows which looked up briefly from grazing.

Fuck, I thought. Fuckety fuck. Why the hell have we stopped?

The minutes ticked by, and I could feel my face growing hot and sweaty. I had only half an hour to get from Peterborough to Retford, and this delay was eating into it. I looked at my phone, which was ringing again. Oh no; it was my wife, Alaleh.

"Darling, thank God I've reached you."

"What's wrong?" I asked. "Where are you?"

"I'm at Vikram's, having my horoscope cast and a free tarot reading."

I groaned. Vikram was a professional astrologer, palm reader, tarot caster and expert in any other fashionable and magical way of foretelling people's longed-for destinies. Alaleh was desperate to find somebody who would predict when she might conceive.

"He says we will have two children, a girl and a boy."

"Great!" I say. "When?"

"That's just it, Andy. He says today is the most propitious day to conceive. We have to make love, and the sooner the better . . . "

I gulped. "Well, I'm on my way to a business meeting at the moment, so it will have to wait."

"It can't wait, Andy," she wailed. "Vikram says the next three hours are uniquely propitious for the conception of a son. A son, think about it . . . It's what you've always wanted, and he's waiting there now for us to conceive him this afternoon!"

I couldn't get my mind round the idea of our yet-to-be created son somehow observing his own creation, but I thought – as I always did during these conversations – of sitting in the stands at West Ham with my boy-to-be perched on my shoulders. It always brought a lump to my throat.

"Look, sweetheart, I'm on a train which is stopped in the middle of nowhere and I've got to meet a new client in Peterborough for an important meeting. He wants to invest a shedload of money in the fund. Then, promise you, I'll come straight back . . . " My anniversary shag with Sharon might have to wait . . .

"But that will be hours!" she cried. "It will be too late. Our little son will not come because of your bloody train and your bloody business trip . . . "

Alaleh (who's Persian by the way) hardly ever swore, so I knew she was in deadly earnest. I couldn't think what on earth to say apart from the truth, which could not be said.

"Where is your train? Tell me, and I will drive to join you!" she said with a kind of triumphant enthusiasm.

At that moment there was an announcement from the driver. What with Alaleh in one ear and the Sniffer in the other, I didn't catch it all apart from something about a broken-down train blocking the line ahead. "Where are we?" I asked the Sniffer.

"I haven't a clue," she snapped.

"Between Stevenage and Peterborough," somebody else piped up. *No shit, Sherlock.*

"A few miles south of Huntingdon," somebody else said, more helpfully. I repeated this information to Alaleh, who was now hyperventilating at the other end of the line.

"And where is Huntingdon?" I asked.

"South of Peterborough . . . but we could be leaving any minute," someone replied.

The Sniffer shook her head vigorously. I cupped my hand

over the phone. "Well it's not north of it, is it?" I asked her, waspishly. She shook her head again.

"No, but we won't be moving yet – they said we could be here an hour . . . "

"Oh shit," I said, exasperated.

"What has happened? What is wrong with you?" Alaleh shouted from the other end of the phone.

I counted to five, waiting for my pulse to slow down. "We could be here a while," I told her, trying to sound calm, and then I gasped for air. We were both hyperventilating now.

"Calm down, *joon-am*, Alaleh will come to you. I am coming now, my darling, be ready for me. I want you so badly, *janedel-am, shereen-am* . . . "

"Just wait!" I shouted, but the phone had gone dead. I rang back but she did not pick up, so I texted her. We are leaving in ten minutes, next stop Peterborough, better wait at home, will return soonest. The trouble is, once Alaleh makes up her mind there is no turning back.

Alaleh and I have been married for ten years. Her parents' families both fled to Britain when the Ayatollah took over. They were both wealthy hoteliers in Teheran, with ski chalets in the mountains. Her father ran a chain of Persian restaurants in the West End and Kensington which his father had established in the 1980s. Her mother was active in the Persian diaspora, helping families who had problems and sitting on various charitable committees. Both fairly secular, although nominally Muslim, they were unconcerned at Alaleh marrying out of their faith and kin. I like them, always have done, and admire their business acumen. They like the fact I make big money in the City. They know I'm not married to Alaleh for her money. Everything is almost perfect, except for the lack of grandchildren. *Babies would complete our family*, they plead. Her father insisted on paying for the fertility treatment. Trouble is I reckon they think it's my fault that we don't have kids, that there's something wrong with me which makes me less than a man. I sometimes think that myself. If I'm honest (well, I am honest occasionally), it's probably why I took up with Sharon – to prove I can be a man without the pressure of trying to have children. I thought it might rub off on my relationship with Alaleh. I know what you're thinking: *Who are you kidding?* But let me tell you, there aren't many things more stressful than having sex to order . . . I feel a bit like a male Anne Boleyn, desperately trying to produce a son and dreading each negative pregnancy test. Not exactly fantastic for the libido . . .

I began to feel more depressed than exasperated. The train wasn't moving. The wind was ruffling the trees outside. A few gulls wheeled behind a tractor. And, unless we set off soon, I would be seriously late meeting Micky with the prospect of Alaleh turning up at any moment to have sex. Oh yeah, and Sharon was expecting me for our anniversary dinner with a nice present. Not to mention my starving old Mum. I wished I'd stayed in the office.

The phone pinged again. This time it was Micky. Another text: Im waiting. Where are you? Our meeting was due to start in ten minutes. I could sense his anxiety like a bad smell. It felt almost cruel to deprive him of the hope that I was only minutes away. No good. He had to be told. I was too cowardly to phone him, so I texted: Train delayed. Stuck outside Peterborough. Hoping to move soon. Alright, not totally honest, but what would *you* have done in my shoes? Better to let him down gently . . .

I put the phone on vibrate and waited. Within seconds it started to quiver, stopped, then started again. With luck he'd think we're on the move and in a tunnel. I looked out of the window, half expecting to see Alaleh walking beside the track in her nightie, peering up at the windows trying to spot me. Then I looked at the case, lying there innocently and bristling with notes.

The mobile quivered frantically. This time I answered.

It wasn't Micky but Dennis from the office, a fellow trader. I sighed with relief. He started rabbiting on about the audit and some unnamed colleague who might have done something a bit out of order. *You naughty boy*, Dennis, I thought, certain he was describing his own actions.

"Sounds dodgy to me," I said. "Some people might even call it fraud, although this anonymous trader would probably have covered his tracks at least well enough to keep the auditors off the scent. Listen, Dennis, I'm on a train *en route* to a business meeting."

"Well what would you do?" he whined, obviously alarmed by my comments.

"I can't discuss it now. Let's talk about it over a beer at lunch tomorrow." I hung up, and noticed the Sniffer was looking at me with unusual interest. I looked at my phone to avoid her gaze. Why couldn't people leave me alone?

"You're talking about fraud," she said. "That's very interesting . . . "

"No, you've got the wrong end of the stick," I butted in, sensing danger. "We were talking about a TV programme, on last night – some bloke at a Japanese bank."

She looked at me blankly, then frowned. "No, *you've* got the wrong end of the stick," she said. "I'm only interested because I need to commit one, not because of what you or your pals may have done. It's just that you look the kind of bloke who understands this sort of thing." A rather sly look stole over her face.

This conversation was starting to hack me off. "Look," I said, "I don't know anything about fraud. It was just a TV programme. If you want to find out about fraud, talk to a fraudster. There are enough of them around."

With which I took yesterday's *FT*, held it up between us and pretended to read the front page. Then I looked at her brown shoes, and a fresh dose of anxiety began to prickle my scalp. Something about them unsettled me. *Don't tell me I've been talking to a PC. Please, no, just my luck to sit opposite a* very *plain-clothes plod.* Was it pure coincidence, or did she know what was in the case? Was I under surveillance?

My heart was thumping like the clappers. I told myself to chillax. If she sensed my panic, she'd know for sure she was on to something. Calmness. Insouciance. Coolness under pressure. That's what people always said about me. *When all around are losing their heads, Andy is at his most self-possessed, ready to make the right decision. Ice-cold Andy. Dead-eye Andy. The snake. The fox. Ready to pounce.* Not somebody scared by a pair of sensible shoes.

There was an announcement. We would be moving soon. And stopping at Huntingdon, for those who wished to use the facilities or make a connection. I wondered whether there might be a short cut from Huntingdon to Retford. To save a bit of time. Then my phone quivered again. Much more activity and the battery would run out.

It was a text. From Micky's phone. You are late. Very late. Your friend Micky should have told you not to keep me waiting. He is in the boot of his car which I am driving. We will be in the car park. Your friend is getting anxious.

I read it, read it again, then shut my eyes. Maybe I had passed out and was having a bad dream. I opened my eyes again. It was still there. The words hadn't changed. I lowered my paper and looked at the Sniffer, who was pouting petulantly. For a millisecond, I thought of sharing my dilemma with her. Perhaps she could arrange for the nasty man to be arrested and my friend to be released, on condition of anonymity. For the public good. But I could almost see a pair of handcuffs being snapped around my wrists. *Don't be stupid.*

I began chewing a Minto. Vigorously, like Alex Ferguson. Then calmness descended on me. The train rumbled forward, normality seemed to have been restored. My pulse slowed

170

down. My brain slipped into gear and I had a welcome rational thought. If this woman was really a plod, and if she knew (how?) that I was conveying money for a criminal enterprise (or so the charge sheet might start), she would follow me to my meeting where we could all be nabbed. So meeting Mr Menace and poor Micky would be a short step to a long stay at Her Majesty's Pleasure. If she didn't follow me, then maybe she wasn't a plod – unless there was a whole team of them on the train. I looked warily at my fellow passengers who all looked disconcertingly normal, well as much as anybody does.

Rational thought number two. This little enterprise had already gone pear-shaped. The deal was I give the money to Micky. So I should demand to see Micky, like some sort of kidnap exchange. And not in front of Mr Menace.

Thought number three (this is becoming like an office memo). What if Alaleh is waiting for me at Peterborough station? She'd tell me nothing is more important than making a son. Micky's plight would cut no ice, assuming I wanted to tell her, which didn't seem such a bright idea. There's parts of my life which are strictly between me and me.

While all these thoughts were forming an orderly queue in my brain, PC Sniffer piped up. "You seem to have a lot of worries."

*Oh dear*, I thought, *oh dear oh dear. She's fishing.* "If you must know," I said, "I'm worried about missing a meeting with a client." Half-truths are always better than whole lies.

"Really? Poor you," she said matily. "Shame you're so preoccupied. I think you could really help me."

"Well, I can't, I need to prep for my meeting. And I really know nothing about fraud."

"But you're a banker, aren't you?" she asked, knowingly.

*Oh no*, I groaned inwardly. *She knows what's in the case.* "Not at all," I said. "I work for an insurance company, if you must know."

She looked down from my perspiring face to my red braces and shook her head. It seemed I was fooling nobody.

The train slowed to a crawl as we slid into Huntingdon. After it had stood on the platform for a while I acted on impulse; I took my case and strode to the exit, waiting for her to follow me. As I stood by the door I looked across to the other platform; it was almost empty, apart from a few bemused people wondering why an Intercity train had stopped. I scanned the faces on both platforms. No uniformed police. *OK, go for it*, I told myself and jumped down. A few other people had got off, looking for the nearest toilet. But not her; she was still on the train. I hesitated, wondering whether to get back on, and stood there for a few minutes in a kind of coma of irresolution. The big diesel began to hum, there was a whistle, some passengers rushed from the loo waving at the guard and clambered back on. The train slid smoothly away with a staccato *whoosh* as each carriage went by.

I was almost alone on the platform now, with my case and my mobile, apart from some guys in anoraks who were scribbling in their notebooks or pouring themselves tea from flasks. One or two passengers emerged from the loo, blinking in the light, looking bemused at the absence of the train. Others had ambled off to the taxi rank. As the noise of the train receded, you could hear birdsong as the sky began to darken. My mobile emitted a faint squawk and flashed the message Your battery is very low. Please connect to a charger. Then the screen went black. I didn't care. I was almost relieved. I couldn't take any more hassle.

I walked to the car park, looking for a taxi rank. I didn't know where I was going to go. Just somewhere, anywhere. I walked behind two cars, parked by the exit. One was a Polo with a little old man inside, plucking hairs from his nostrils. The other was an old Rover, circa 1954. It looked so perfect it could have just glided out of a show room. The only slightly weird feature was a dull knocking from the boot.

Ah, you're saying, that will be Micky. Well, don't jump to conclusions. Micky wouldn't be seen dead in a classic car, unless it was a sports car. In any case, he tends to drive what's in stock. And a Rover 90 is definitely not his style. As for the knocking, well, maybe Huntingdon is one of those dark towns where lots of stuff goes on and being stuck in the boot of a car is no big deal. I mean, it might *not* be Micky. As one of my old bosses used to say, *It's the facts that matter* and Micky's presence was, well, *conjectural*, if you know what I mean. If it *was* him, how did Mr Menace know I'd get off at Huntingdon?

That really put the wind up me. Maybe I was being tracked somehow, the way police do with mobile phones. Pity the damn thing hadn't died on the train. I started to breathe heavily, as if I'd been running uphill. The quietness around me suddenly felt creepy, like something really nasty was about to happen.

Somebody came out of the station, a small guy in a blue pullover, cravat and blazer. Perfect. The Rover driver. They all wore cravats in the 50s. Probably smoked a pipe too. This guy's obviously into playing the part. He's even got a little clipped moustache. Then a thought worms its way into my consciousness. He was on the train, diagonally opposite, window seat, reading *Classic Cars* and mumbling into his phone every now and then. He'd looked at me a few times, but nothing out of the ordinary. And now he's looking at me again.

I nod. He nods. Goes to the driver's door of the Rover. Then there's a thump from inside the boot. I look at him enquiringly.

"Sounds like your dog wants to come out," I say, thinking wouldn't it be nice if it was a dog rather than a person.

"If I let 'im out, e'd bite your balls off." He pats the boot and stares at me, and the case.

"Best keep him there then," I say, trying to maintain a jocular tone.

His eyes travel up and down me, as though he is sizing me up for a new suit. He looks pointedly at the case.

"Whatcha got in there then?"

"Papers," I reply, a bit too quickly.

"Papers eh? Lots of notes and stuff?" He winks. My ticker goes from 3/4 to 6/8.

I'm trying to place his accent. Cinema Cockney. Bob Hoskins *circa* 1985. Not quite the real thing.

He goes round to the driver's side, climbs in and shuts the door with a heavy clunk. That's alright then, I think, he's going to drive off now. Probably going to take his dog for a walk. I wonder why the dog doesn't bark. Well, some don't. Anyway, that's not my concern. The point is, I've still got the case. I just need a taxi to take me somewhere. And a phone charger.

I tell myself to man up, to stop panicking. I'm just another businessman with a case, minding my own business and hoping other people will mind theirs. The man in the Rover is on his mobile again. He keeps peering at his wing mirror. In which I'm reflected. I turn to walk away and find myself walking towards a tall gangly man in a dinner jacket, jeans and shades. He's doing up his flies in a leisurely fashion, button by button. And staring at me, unblinking. I turn ninety degrees and start walking across the car park. We have a saying in trading, *Always walk to the exit*. I'm trying my damndest to maintain a walk but my legs have a mind of their own and I break into a stuttering trot, like a nervous horse in dressage.

"Oi!" a voice shouts behind me. "Andy, isn't it?"

I move up the gears into a canter, raising my legs to lengthen my stride. Behind me, another clunk and the Rover fires up and whines into first gear. A taxi draws into the car park and I wave at it, but it carries on. I curse the passenger for their selfishness.

The car's alongside me now. The back window winds down. It's the gangly man. "Need a lift, Andy?"

I shake my head, and keep running. Sweat is breaking out all over me. I'm out of condition and gasping for air. "That case is slowing you down, Andy. Those notes are a bit heavy, eh?"

I slow down to a canter. It's no good. My legs feel like lead.

174

I come to a halt. The Rover stops too, and the driver gets out. He is holding a gun and it's pointing at me.

"Put that bloody thing away," I gasp, trying to catch my breath.

"Get in and we'll talk about it." He opens the back door, and I see that the gangly man's got a shooter too.

I know what I *should* do. Throw the case at him and run. After all, he must be after the money, not me. "And what's £50,000?" I can feel Mum and Alaleh and her parents asking, "compared to us?"

The trouble is, when you work with money, you've got to respect it. You don't give it away. I climbed into the car, muttering my apologies to those I love.

The gangly man put his gun into a carrier bag, leaned back and smiled pleasantly.

"Nice to meet you, Andy." He proffered a hand, which I shook. "You can call me Eric."

"Hi Eric," I said weakly, trying to pretend this was just another business meeting.

"Let me introduce you to my driver, Stanley". Stanley looked round with a lopsided grin. Close up I could see he was wearing a toupée. I wondered how old he was.

"Where are we going?" I asked. "I'm meeting my wife in Peterborough . . . "

"Very nice," Stanley said. "Going shopping?"

"Well, sort of. We're staying overnight in a hotel."

"Anniversary is it? A little treat?"

"Well, sort of . . . "

We all lapsed into silence. We were driving through a dead flat landscape on a dead straight road, towards a huge blue sky turning a dark shade of indigo. Fenland farm houses reared up like ships with telegraph poles for masts. The declining sun lit up a dyke in a long strip of silver. The landscape felt increasingly gloomy, like it would swallow us up.

"Nice motor," I said, as cheerfully as I could.

"Last for ever," Stanley piped up, "if you look after them. They built the fuckers to last . . . "

"Language, Stanley," Eric chided. "No way to talk about such a faithful old retainer . . . "

"Sorry," Stanley mumbled sheepishly.

"I prefer something newer and quicker," I said, feeling somehow that if I could keep them on such anodyne subjects, we could avoid any nastiness.

"I'm sure you do. We prefer cars which appreciate. Choose carefully, and you've got yourself a nice little earner," Eric said, stroking the wooden window trim.

At that moment, there was a muffled voice from the boot.

"Calm down, *Michael*," Eric said. "We've got your friend Andy. And Andy's got the case which I sincerely hope contains the money. That's what we're all here for . . . "

More muffled shouting from the rear.

"I think he wants to go to the toilet, boss," Stanley said.

"Oh dear, oh dear. We can't have him soiling himself, can we?" Eric chuckled.

"Shall I stop?" Stanley asked.

"What the hell for?" Eric exclaimed. "We're not on a coach outing, Stanley."

Silence once again. A faint odour of urine comes from behind us.

The landscape begins to change. There are more trees, houses, signs of civilization. We pass a sign which says *Peterborough 5 miles*.

I feel like I'm in a film, a cross between an 80s gangster movie and an Ealing comedy. The question is which? Bob Hoskins. Where do I remember that voice? Ah yes, *The Long Good Friday*. At the end, he's in a car leaving a London hotel. He thinks it's his driver, but it's not. It's the IRA. A shiver comes over me. Then I think of *Goodfellas*. The mad one attacks a

Mafia made-man in a bar. They stuff him into the boot with a spade and drive into the desert. Is that what's in store for Micky? I wish I could remember the Ealing comedies better to cheer myself up.

"Tell you what," Eric says, "why don't we open that case of yours and count the money?"

I agree, and open the case. Eric smiles as he handles the first wad of notes. We develop a system. He checks how much is in each wad, and I count the wads. Fifty notes per wad, fifty wads; very symmetrical. We fall into a rhythm. He's totally absorbed. We are coming into Peterborough now, stopping and starting in the rush hour traffic.

"Where do you want dropping off?" Eric asks when we finish.

I look at him. Is this an innocent question? Or something more sinister?

"Are you going to whack me?" I ask, remembering my Mafia slang.

"Stanley," Eric says sharply. "Did you hear what Andy asked? He wants to know whether we're going to whack him."

"What does he take us for?" Stanley asks, with theatrical surprise.

"Look, can we cut out the crap?" I ask. "What's happening to the money? And to us? We were meant to meet in Peterborough – and Micky was going to give the money to you, not me . . . "

"Bit late for that," Eric says. "You should have stayed on the train. The boss is very cross."

"Well, I found myself sitting opposite a copper," I said. "At least I think she was . . . "

"Is that right, Stanley?"

"Well, I can usually smell 'em, but I didn't smell nothing."

"Anyway," Eric said, "the boss doesn't like to take chances. So as soon as we knew the train was delayed, he told me and Stanley to drive over to Huntingdon. Just in case."

"And Micky?"

"Well, we thought best to keep you together."

I felt none the wiser. I looked out and saw a sign for the station.

"Can we drop you off here?" Eric asked,

"But what about Micky?" I said. I was beginning to feel a bit guilty about him.

"He's coming back with us to Retford. Don't worry, we'll clean him up."

So that was that. They dropped me in the station car park, minus the money of course. But Eric said the deal would still go through and I'd get it back in a few weeks. *Probably.*

I stepped out of the car and watched them drive away. I was alive. Minus £50k, which might or might not come back. Ordinarily, that would have pissed me off big time. But I was alive. I had survived. As the fear ebbed, an acute love of life welled up in me like desire. I needed to find Alaleh, and we needed to find a hotel. She was right. This was a propitious day. And there she was, parked up in the Beamer. She leapt out and hugged me. We held each other, for much longer than normal.

"Praise be," she cried. "We have found each other just in time."

"Sorry I'm late," I said. "I had a bit of bother . . . "

# Facing the music
by Vicky Trelinska

"GOD," muttered Alice, frowning. "Another message. Six of them. Hasn't she anything better to do?" She shoved the phone into her jacket pocket. Her mother could wait. She must catch the train. She had already missed the one her mother told her to get. She checked the departures board. It would be alright: there was still ten minutes to go before it left.

Finding a seat by a window she threw her suit carrier on to the luggage rack, flopped down and dumped her music case on the seat beside her, hoping it would deter anyone from sitting there.

She took out her phone and scrolled through the messages. Did you catch the 14:08 train? Is it on time? Did you remember to bring the pink dress? Have you got your gloves? I'll be at Ptbrh at 14:59 Answer me. Alice sighed. She had better send something to keep her mother quiet. Delayed leaving school missed the 1408 got the 1508 arrives at 1559.

This was true as far as it went. She *had* been at school and she *was* on the 15:08 train to Peterborough which arrived at 15:59, but she left out the reason why she was delayed.

"Excuse me, is this seat free?" Alice looked up at the slim grey-haired woman who was smiling at her and pointing to the seat opposite.

"Yes it is." Alice sat up and moved her outstretched legs. She watched the woman put a large bag on the overhead rack, and was disappointed when she took care not to put her bag near Alice's suit carrier.

There was nothing Alice would have liked better than to see the horrible, pink frilly dress in the suit carrier crushed. Her mother insisted she wear it for the piano competition that afternoon. When she had protested, her mother said, "'But it's lovely. I don't understand why you don't like it. You look so pretty in it. The judges will be impressed by such a young, talented pianist."

Alice did not understand. The judges always knew how old contestants were from their entry forms. At sixteen, she felt she should be wearing something trendy.

Her phone rang. "What?" Alice snapped at her mother.

"That's no way to speak to me. Why aren't you on the train you were supposed to catch? Why were you delayed at school? They'd agreed you could leave at lunch-time. Now you'll have to change on the train. There won't be time to change at the venue. The last thing we needed was to be in a rush. What were you thinking leaving school so late? I bought you an open ticket hoping you'd be able to catch an earlier train not so that you could dawdle and catch a later one. Suppose the train is late? Your slot is at five-fifteen so we have only an hour and a quarter to get to Oundle, even if the train is on time. I shouldn't have gone to Peterborough today. I should have taken the day off."

Alice had stopped listening to her mother. She looked out of the window and watched the last passengers rushing for the train, wondering why one woman was wearing flip-flops in March.

She realised her mother had paused for breath. "It'll be fine. Stop panicking. These competitions always run late. It isn't that far from Peterborough. I'm not changing on the train. I'll look an idiot in a long pink dress at this time of day."

Alice was determined not to be seen in public in a dress

which she felt was more suitable for a five-year-old's birthday party than for a sixteen-year-old taking part in an international piano competition.

"It's not fine. If you change on the train you'll have time to warm up on the practice piano. This is a very important competition. With all the concerts and recitals you'll have if you win you won't need to go to music college. You could study privately with Reichert in Vienna instead. I'm sure she'd take you on. You should walk through the first round but only if you are mentally prepared and focused."

"I will be," Alice said, though she knew she did not want to study, neither with Reichert – who had a reputation for being a tyrant – nor in Vienna. If she went anywhere, it would be to study with a Chopin specialist in Warsaw.

"Are your hands warm? Have you got your gloves on? You know how cold your hands get."

"Yes, my hands are warm. Yes, I have my gloves," she said, looking at her music case. She would have to put them on before she left the train or her mother would rant all the way to Oundle and the car heater would be turned full on. Hot and sweaty hands were just as bad as cold hands.

"Why were you delayed?"

"I told you. I got held up at school."

"I shall have to speak to them, though it's probably not worth it as you're leaving after your GCSEs next term." Alice thought back to the talk she had been to at lunch-time about degrees and careers in science. If her mother had not mapped out a career for her as a solo pianist she would do science 'A' levels and then an engineering degree. It sounded fascinating and would mean doing her favourite subjects, maths and physics.

"I can go to the Prom after the exams, can't I?" Alice had already seen the dress she wanted to wear in Coast. It was black, elegant and sexy. She had her heart set on going to this end-of-term event, held every year with the boys' school, and be like the other girls. She did not have much time to socialise: after practising and school work, she had little spare time. She often had only her mother for company. The other girls moaned about their siblings but Alice thought how much she would like to have a brother or sister. She was allowed out with friends on a Saturday evening provided she had finished her homework, done her practising and was not performing somewhere. She often thought the girls at school only wanted to be friends to show her off so they could say, *Have you heard of Alice Barnwell? Yes, she is very talented. We're at school together. She's a friend of mine.* Alice had not minded this until a few years ago but, gradually, she had grown to resent it and wanted to be an ordinary girl, not a mascot, although she supposed it was better than having no friends.

"If you win this competition, I'll doubt you'll have time." Alice sighed. Was the only way to go to the dance not to win the competition? It was not in her nature to play badly on purpose. She was ambitious and highly competitive, and she loved the attention, praise and kudos of winning. "I'll pick you up at Peterborough. Got to go. I've left an important meeting."

"OK. Bye." Alice looked out of the window at the London suburbs speeding past. The woman opposite was on the phone and Alice could not help overhearing.

"Can you or Dad pick me up at York? . . . I'll ring you just before I get in. I thought we'd get fish and chips on the way home. I'm too tired to cook. . . . It was interesting. The seminar on geriatrics was particularly good . . . I took Simon out for a meal last night. He sends his love and he'll be home for Easter . . . I'll tell you all his news when I see you. Bye love."

Alice's mother never called her 'love'. Lately they seemed unable to talk without arguing and getting cross with each other. It would be nice to have the sort of conversation other people had with their mothers. If only her mother would listen to her instead of giving her orders all the time. She knew she owed

183

her mother everything and doubted she would have developed her talent and won a scholarship to the Junior Conservatoire at the age of twelve without her mother pushing her all the way. Alice had been taught by her mother at the beginning. Her mother had been a very good pianist but stopped playing when she went to university. When Alice asked why her mother had stopped playing, she was given a different story each time. *There was no time to practise. There was nowhere to practise. I wasn't that good. I had a repetitive strain injury.* Alice did not know her father – he had left home when her mother was pregnant with her. She had not heard stories about him. Whenever she asked, her mother said she thought he had gone to America and refused to tell her any more.

*It's no good sitting here daydreaming*, Alice thought. *I had better do some work.* That meant going over the thirty-minute programme she was playing in the competition. She took the Bach *Prelude and Fugue* from her music case. There was no problem with that. She had played it so many times she could probably do it standing on her head in the dark. If anything, the problem would be that it was too familiar and she could easily lose concentration and make a mistake.

In the past Alice had not suffered from nerves before a performance but, in the last few months, she had sometimes woken in the night gasping for breath and shaking. She remembered nightmares in which she had forgotten the music or turned up at the wrong concert hall.

Last night she dreamt she was flying, skimming over the stalls in a theatre. She had just started to fly up to the dress circle when she felt something tugging her back down. She looked round to see her mother holding on to her skirt. Alice had said, "Oh, it's you!" and struggled to get out of her mother's grasp. It had taken her a long time to get back to sleep afterwards.

Alice noticed the woman reading *Scientific American*. Alice liked to read it in the school library. If she took it home her mother got annoyed. "You've no time for magazines, you haven't finished your homework," she would say, or, "You haven't time to read, you should be practising." At least her mother couldn't get into the school library.

How nice it would be, Alice thought, to be able to read what she wanted on the train. Instead she had to think about the competition and what she was going to play, go over all the difficult passages in her mind and keep her fingers warm.

She put the Bach away and looked through the Beethoven *Sonata*. That would be fine. She checked the Chopin *Etude in A flat*. It would be easy to take a wrong turn and end up back at the beginning. But it was no good fussing. She put the music away.

Alice checked her watch. The train was on time. Her mother was worrying unnecessarily. Her hands were warm and she was well-prepared. She could sit back and watch the scenery and think about the careers lecture.

Alice imagined studying engineering then travelling round the world building bridges and dams, or blasting through mountains, making tunnels for roads and railways. The woman who had given the talk was enthusiastic and her presentation was really interesting. Alice's science teachers all wanted her to do 'A' levels. It was just her mother who wouldn't hear of it.

She was lost in a daydream where only she knew how to solve a construction problem with a bridge when the train lurched to a halt. The woman's bag was jolted half-off the rack. She stood up and pushed it back, once again taking care to avoid the suit carrier. *Bother*, thought Alice. *Why is it that that dress I hate is never damaged but the things I love, like that blue skirt I bought last summer, always get some sort of stain or mark on them?* Assuming that the train was being held at a red signal, she returned to her daydream. She had just got to the point where she was telling all the men what they needed to do when she became aware of an announcement over the tannoy.

185

"Excuse me," she said to the woman. "What was that announcement?"

The woman looked up from her magazine. "Something about a broken-down train ahead of us and they'll keep us informed."

"Did they say how long it would be?"

"No." Alice thought about sending her mother a text to say there was a delay, but decided against it. If the train started moving soon there would be no point worrying her. She took out her music and looked through the Liszt, checking her watch every now and again. If the train did not get going soon she would be late and her mother would be spiralling out of control, no doubt making it out to be Alice's fault.

It was ten minutes before the next announcement. This time Alice listened.

> **We regret to inform you that we will be unable to move for up to an hour. Engineers are working as fast as possible to clear the other train from the line. Meanwhile we ask for your patience. The buffet car is open.**

Alice went cold. The train would now arrive in Peterborough at five at the earliest. She would be late, but she reassured herself that these competitions never ran on time. It was not her fault the train was delayed so surely they would fit her in at the end of the day, or tomorrow?

She sent her mother a text train delayed A few minutes later her mother rang. "How long is it delayed?" When Alice told her, she screamed, "An hour? Are you sure?"

"That's what they've said."

"That means we can't get there on time."

"Oundle's not far from Peterborough, is it? We won't be very late. I'm sure they'll fit me in."

"I'll try to find out what's happening from the train company.

I'll ring the competition and tell them you're delayed. We'll have to hope they're sympathetic. I can't believe this, Alice. Why didn't you catch the train I told you to?"

Alice cut off the call without answering her mother.

"Is the delay causing a problem for you?" The woman put down her magazine and looked concerned. Alice assumed she had heard her mother shouting. "I'm sorry," the woman continued, "I'm afraid I couldn't help overhearing. Is it important that you get to Oundle?"

"Yes, I suppose it is," Alice replied.

"Is there anything I can do to help?"

"Thanks, but there's nothing anyone can do. I'll just be late, and hopefully my mother will be able to get the judges to hear me at the end of the day."

"Judges?" The woman eyes widened.

"Oh, I'm not in any trouble," said Alice, wondering if the woman thought she was appearing in some sort of juvenile court. "I'm taking part in a piano competition. I won't now be able to get there on time so my mother will explain to the judges what's happened and see if they will hear me later today or tomorrow. It lasts several days so I'm sure they'll fit me in."

The woman looked relieved. "Oh, I see. I'm sure they'll find time to hear you. Such a lovely instrument, the piano. I've never played but all my children learnt when they were at primary school. None of them liked practising, though, and once they were at secondary school I said I wasn't going to pay for lessons if they didn't practise, so they all gave up. We all enjoy listening to piano music. I expect you practise for hours if you're doing a competition."

"I do about six hours a day."

"How do you fit it in with your school work?"

"I get up early and practise before school. I'm allowed to miss some subjects, like games and art, and I'm allowed to practise then."

"It sounds as hard as doing ballet. You must be very good to be given special treatment."

"I go to the Junior Conservatoire on Saturdays but there are plenty there who are as good as I am – or even better. There's a new Chinese boy who started this term and he is younger and more talented."

Alice's phone rang. "I can't get anything out of the train company," said her mother. "The organisers have said they'll fit you in at the end of the day. I just hope this doesn't prejudice them against you. You'll have to change on the train."

"I'm not changing on the train."

"You'll have to."

"The loos are engaged and have been for ages."

"They must be free at some point. Go and queue."

Alice raised her voice. "I'm not wearing that dress on the train."

"Don't argue, Alice, and there's no need to shout. If you'd been on time you wouldn't have to change on the train. No one will mind. It's a very pretty dress." Alice grimaced as her mother carried on. "There'll be no time to warm up. You'll have to go in cold. Keep your gloves on. If you'd done as I said we wouldn't be in this mess. I'll be waiting for you at Peterborough. I'll be in the car at the station entrance so we can make a dash for it. Let me know as soon as the train moves. I'll keep checking the website."

"OK." Alice gritted her teeth and looked out of the window. She felt her eyes filling with tears but she was determined not to cry. She fumbled in her pocket for a tissue.

"Here take this." The woman handed her a pack of tissues. "I'm Greta by the way."

Alice looked at the woman whose open, friendly face and smiling blue eyes inspired confidence. She wondered if Greta would understand about the dress.

"I'm Alice. My mother says they'll hear me at the end of the day. The problem is she wants me to change, now, into the dress I'm wearing. I can't wear it on the train. It's long and pink; I'll look a fool." She paused to blow her nose. "We always argue about it and now because I'm late she's getting cross."

"I'm sure no-one on the train will mind what you're wearing. I saw a woman get on the train wearing flip-flops. You can wear what you like these days and no-one will comment. Don't you like pink?"

"Look at this and you'll see what I mean."

Alice took out her phone and found the *You Tube* film of her playing, pausing on a shot of her in the dress. She passed it to Greta. "There. You see – it's hideous." The dress was pale pink satin with puffed sleeves, a round neckline, a wide sash at the waist tied at the back with a bow and rows of lace frills round the skirt. "I feel like a stick of candy floss in it."

"As my daughter will tell you," said Greta, "I'm no style guru but it doesn't seem quite right for – what are you, sixteen, seventeen?"

"Sixteen."

"I don't think the judges will pay any attention to what you're wearing. Surely they are more interested in how well you play. What are you playing in that film?" Alice handed Greta an earpiece and started the short film of her playing the Chopin *Etude in A flat major*. "It sounds very good to me," said Greta as she returned the earpiece. "Are you playing it today?"

"Yes."

"What happens if you win?"

"There are several rounds to get through before the final but if I win there is a series of recitals and a concerto with one of the orchestras. Agents are invited to the final and also invited to the concerts and there will be a lot of press coverage. If the agents like me they might take me on."

"Good luck then; or should I say break a leg?"

Alice laughed. "Good luck's fine."

Greta returned to her magazine and Alice to her music and they sat in silence. Alice felt happier now that there was at least one person in the world who agreed with her about the dress. After a while, Greta put the *Scientific American* magazine on the seat next to her and took the *British Medical Journal* out of her bag. "May I read it?" Alice pointed to the *Scientific American*, and Greta passed it over to her.

"Keep it. I've finished with it. Are you interested in science?"

"Yes, I love it." Alice leant forward, her eyes glowed with enthusiasm. "I'm doing physics, chemistry and biology for my GCSEs in the summer. I'd like to do science at 'A' level but my mother won't let me." She put the magazine on her knees, sagged back into the seat and folded her arms.

"Why won't she let you? It sounds a good idea to me, but then I'm biased. I did science at school and studied medicine. My husband's a doctor as well and my son is doing biochemistry."

"I'd really love to study engineering at university." Alice uncrossed her arms and started to speak quickly. "We had a really good talk today about careers in science. I liked the sound of jobs in engineering."

"You'd have to do maths and physics."

"I love those subjects."

"Can't you do 'A' levels and *then* decide whether to do science or music? Another two years at school would give you time to make up your mind."

"My mother says I must leave school after GCSEs. I've been offered places in London and New York to study, but I'd rather stay on at school. She told me not to go to the talk today but I did. That meant I had to catch this train and not the earlier one. I'm glad I went to the talk, though, and it would all have been alright if this train hadn't been delayed. She's invested so much in my music that I couldn't disappoint her." Alice shrank back into her seat and turned away from Greta. The spark in her eyes went out.

"Surely your mother wants you to be happy and have a career that you enjoy. If more people followed their hearts rather than their heads I'd have fewer people in my surgery."

"I *am* happy." But now Alice had said it she was not so sure. "I've always loved playing the piano but I love science just as much." Now, thinking about it, she wondered if she did not love science more. Did she want to have the career as a concert pianist her mother had planned for her? She knew she was good but there were others at the Junior Conservatoire who were just as good as her and that new Chinese boy was way ahead of her. Whenever she expressed any doubts her mother told her not to be silly, that she was just being neurotic. She reminded Alice about the prizes she'd won, how well the critics had reviewed the concerto she'd performed with the Youth Orchestra, that the CDs she had made always sold well at any recital she gave.

Alice's phone rang. "Are you moving yet?"

"No."

"Have they said when you will be?"

"No."

"You're not being very helpful, Alice."

"Well they haven't said anything, OK? I'll ring when they do."

"Don't get worked up. You need to keep calm. Start focusing on the competition and getting mentally prepared."

"Alright," Alice hung up.

"Do you know," said Greta, "that you frown every time you talk about music? You seemed happier when we were talking about science."

"I do enjoy science."

"Do it then."

"I can't . . . I can't let my mother down. It's been her dream."

"Not yours?"

Alice didn't answer. She turned away and looked out of the window at the branches of the trees, which were starting to turn from the dead brown and grey of winter to the yellow-green of spring. *Greta made it sound so easy*, she thought. *Just do science*. It would make a mockery of her life so far, wasting the sacrifices she had made and all the time and effort she and her mother had put in. She looked back at Greta.

"You don't understand. It's not that easy."

"Nothing worthwhile is easy. Look at what you've achieved with your piano playing. That can't have been easy but I expect you've found that the rewards were great. Doing 'A' levels will at least give you time to think what you want to do with your life and not what your mother wants you to do. It's your life, not hers."

Another announcement. They were on the move but would make an unscheduled stop at Huntingdon. She sent her mother a text.

Some of the other passengers were collecting their things together, preparing to get off at Huntingdon. She supposed it was too late now for them to get to wherever they were going and that they had decided it would be simpler to go straight back to London. She picked up the *Scientific American*. *How nice*, she thought, flicking through the pages, *to be able to get off and go home*. She could watch TV, do her homework and read Greta's *Scientific American*. No more competition, no need to practise, no need to keep calm or focused or be mentally prepared and, most important of all, no need to wear a long, pink dress. Those last five words of Greta's repeated in her head. *It's your life, not hers . . .*

The train arrived at Huntingdon and Alice leapt to her feet. "I'm going."

"Going? Where?"

"Home." She brushed past Greta's knees. "I'm sorry," she apologised as she tripped over Greta's feet in her rush to get off the train.

"What about the competition?"

"I'm not doing it. Bye," she called back as she rushed for the door.

"Are you sure?"

But Alice had not heard. She was already out of the train. *Freedom*, she thought. *Just do science? Why not?* No one could make her play the piano. They might drag her to the keyboard and shackle her to it but they could not make her fingers move.

Somehow she had to convince her mother that she was burnt out, that playing the piano was becoming a drudge and she needed a break. She must make her mother understand that she needed time to think about where her life was going. Two more years at school doing 'A' levels would give her that. She would not stop playing the piano, she would just do less – no more competitions, no more recitals. After 'A' levels she still might go to music college, but by then she would know whether it was to be science or music.

Her mother would go off like a Chinese firecracker, spitting and exploding in all directions. Alice knew she would have to be very determined to stand up to her. It would be difficult and she would have to face up to the arguments and rows that would follow this decision but surely her mother would grant her two more years at school? As Greta said, *nothing worthwhile is easy* and it was *her* life, not her mother's.

As the train started to pull out of the station, Alice looked for Greta. She was at the window, waving something in each hand. *Oh, no!* Alice gasped. She'd left the suit carrier and music case on the train. She laughed and waved the *Scientific American*.

She texted her mother: all fine, gone home, not doing the comp then switched off her phone and went to find the train back to London, all traces of a frown gone and Greta's words *It's your life, not your mother's* playing in her head like a mantra.

# Connection
## by Phil Tysoe

"DO you want a hand with that?" he asked, nodding towards the case she was wheeling up the aisle. She shook her head.

"It's alright, thanks. I can manage," she muttered as she picked up the case and rose on tiptoes to place it on the overhead rack opposite his table. As he watched her struggle his eyes were drawn to the small of her back, her jumper lifting as she stretched to reveal a small butterfly tattoo nestled against the curve of her spine. He averted his eyes as she turned back towards him. "Anyone sitting there?" she asked, pointing at the seats opposite him. He shook his head and she slid in next to the aisle, diagonally across from him. She self-consciously pulled at the bottom of her jumper, smoothing it down firmly with her hands as if aware that he'd been watching her, then folded her arms across her chest and stared out of the window. He considered complimenting her on the tattoo but thought better of it and turned his attention back to his phone.

She gazed out of the window, briefly closing her eyes and enjoying the quiet of the carriage; it was a relief to be away from that snivelling, sniffing woman. Moving seats hadn't changed the view though, static for the last fifteen minutes since the train had stopped. Hadn't changed the view save she couldn't look at it without also seeing her new travelling companion, either directly or in glimpses reflected in the glass. Wedged in the corner of his seat and against the window. Without staring more openly she could only catch snapshots of him, an impression. Short, sandy, untidy hair. Loosened tie. Turning a pen over and over between fingers hovering over an unopened notebook, his face set in a frown, puzzled rather than sad.

He glanced up and looked directly at her. He smiled then broke eye contact. She had green eyes, mouth set in a firm line, long dark hair tied up in a ponytail. As she turned to look out of the window he noticed the line of her jaw and traced it down to her neck, exposed above the open 'V' of her jumper. The tannoy broke the silence.

> We regret to inform you that we will be unable to move for up to an hour. Engineers are working as fast as possible to clear the other train from the line. Meanwhile, we ask for your patience. The buffet car is open.

She sighed and looked at her watch before pulling a phone from her pocket. She prodded at it and sighed again. "Sorry to bother you but I don't suppose you've got a phone charger with you?"

"Afraid not," he answered. "Looks like we've got different phones anyway. If you need to call someone about the delay you can borrow mine if you want."

"Really? Thanks, that'd be great. I just need to tell my parents I'm running late."

"Travelling home?"

"Something like that."

He passed her his phone and she made a brief call, turning her head and cupping her mouth behind her hand. "No, you don't need to pick me up. Really, I'm OK . . . Please don't worry about doing anything for dinner, I'll sort myself out . . . I'll get a cab." She slid the phone back across the table.

He looked at her hands, the long fingers ending in quick-bitten nails, as she sat back in her seat, rubbing her eyes. "Long day?" he asked. She nodded but didn't reply. She'd moved seats looking for somewhere quiet, somewhere to think. In truth she'd spent most of the day thinking, running the same questions through her mind as she'd sat on various trains making their way from Paris, across London, and up to her old family home in Peterborough. The same questions and no answers; just a sense of failure and disappointment. This journey home had never been part of the plan. She looked at him again.

"I'm sorry. You must think I'm being really rude," she offered. "It's been a long day. I'm travelling back from Paris."

"No need to apologise, that sounds pretty tiring," he said. There was a pause before he added, "I'm Jack, by the way. Nice to meet you."

"Thanks again for the phone, Jack. Nice to meet you too. I'm Kate." She closed her eyes and leant back in the seat. "I'm so tired."

Jack continued to chat, just small talk about the delay and how busy it had been in London earlier, and, despite herself, Kate began to respond. Just nods and murmurs of agreement at first, but slowly she was drawn into conversation. He was easy company and she found that she'd missed the sound of her own language, missed conversation where there wasn't that briefest of gaps between her thoughts and the translation. The fluency fraction. Or *fraction de fluidité*, as she'd once tried to explain to a group of new French friends, following a few too many glasses of wine, after the move to Paris. They'd laughed and one of them had poured her another glass. She'd spent the next six months with him.

"What would 'sassy' mean to you?" asked Jack, interrupting her thoughts.

"Sassy?" repeated Kate. "Depends on the context I guess."

"OK," said Jack. "On a dating profile. I keep getting recommended women who are sassy, independent, and smart." He held up the phone she'd borrowed earlier, open on a web page headed *Soul Mates*.

"Sure you can cope with that?" asked Kate with a smile.

"No, I'm not *exactly* . . . " laughed Jack. "But sassy could mean all sorts of things. If it means someone who likes some lively banter then I might be alright but if it's shorthand for someone who's high maintenance, with a biting tongue and a cruel wit then it's a whole different matter."

"I'm fairly sure no-one who actually wanted a date would describe themselves as 'a high maintenance cruel wit with a biting tongue' on their profile . . . "

"No, sure, but is that within the bounds of what it could mean? That's the question," mused Jack. "Is it a word you think you would use?"

Kate let her gaze drift outside to the fields but she could still see him in the glass, looking at her intently. Turning her head towards the window her own translucent reflection crept into view, mirroring how she felt: indistinct, dislocated, a little blurred round the edges. 'Sassy' might have been a word she'd have used once, confident and sure in who she was, but not so much now. She wasn't even sure she liked the word any more. It was like 'feisty'. Why was it only women who were ever sassy or feisty? As if being lively and bold and confident were so beyond the boundaries of what was expected from a woman that there had to be special words ascribed to it. 'Spirited.' That was another one. Feisty and spirited. Like a horse or something. She turned back to Jack. "No, it's not a word I think I'd use," she said. "I think it's something people put because they think other people want to hear it."

"Like everyone says they've got a great sense of humour?" asked Jack.

"Exactly like that," said Kate. "Or like everyone says they enjoy taking long romantic walks or visiting art galleries or keeping in shape or socializing with a wide circle of friends. It's all shorthand isn't it? Here's my profile: I am nice, cultured, physically fit and not a social pariah."

"It's the profile pictures that get me. Everyone's a picture of health, permanently smiling, and radiating an air of calm contentment. Where are all the desperate selfies, tear-smudged mascara or dishevelled five-day beard because you haven't left the house for a week after your last relationship ended in the usual bitterness and recrimination?"

"Oh you should definitely change your picture to one of those," said Kate. "Mascara would be a strong look for you." Jack laughed and rubbed the corner of his eye. Kate tilted her head and pulled at her ponytail. "I particularly like the ones where it's clearly a photo chopped in half. You know what I mean?"

Jack nodded. "Where some old flame was in the frame before they were extinguished with a pair of scissors . . . "

"Can you extinguish something with scissors?"

"Words were never really my thing," he acknowledged. "Maybe like this . . . " He flipped open the notepad that sat on the table between them and deftly sketched a fire extinguisher, a pair of scissors cutting through its short hose.

"A bit literal?" frowned Kate.

"Everyone's a critic! How about this then?" He drew a pair of candles, the first with a flickering flame, suggested by a couple of spare, precise lines that almost made the static drawing dance. Beneath it he placed a closed pair of scissors with the handles elongated to look like a heart. The second candle's wick was snipped, the flame now just a wisp of smoke, and the pair of scissors beneath it was open, heart-like handles pulled apart. Kate smiled, smoothing her hair again with her hand.

"That works. You're good."

"Thanks. Like I say, words were never really my thing.

Probably why I never seem to get anywhere with this online dating thing."

"You having trouble writing your profile?"

"Something like that. Having trouble getting anyone to reply to my profile might be more accurate."

"Read it to me," said Kate, sitting forward in her seat, resting her elbows on the table, chin in her hands. "Perhaps I can help."

"It's not very interesting. It just says: *Slim, athletic man, 28, enjoys films, books, restaurants, and meeting up with friends. WLTM woman 25-35.*"

"WLTM?"

"Would love to meet. I thought I should read it as written."

"You forgot to mention that you've got a good sense of humour . . . "

"Let me finish? *WLTM woman 25-35. GSOH. Looking for someone fun and friendly.*"

"GSOH, of course. Well, you *sound* nice enough," said Kate. "Doesn't tell me much about you though. Not *really* about you."

"You reckon it's just stuff I think other people want to hear?"

"I don't know. Is it?"

"Maybe. I don't know. I guess I'm banking on my photo to look suitably appealing on its own."

"Is it one with an extinguished old flame?" asked Kate, picking up Jack's drawings. He looked away and rubbed his hand through his hair, scratching at the back of his head. Kate put the paper back on the table and there was an awkward silence.

Jack spoke first. "What would yours say then?"

"My what?" asked Kate.

"Your dating profile," said Jack. "I'm not saying you need one but, if you had one and could strip out all the clichés and the shorthand and the things we write to show people what we think they want to see, what would yours say?"

"Ah, I don't know if I want to do that," sighed Kate. She felt like all that was left was cliché. Mid-twenties – who was she kidding? Nearly late-twenties – and moving back in with her parents because the great *Parisienne* dream had turned into a nightmare. What was left to say? *I had everything I thought I wanted? It all turned to merde?*

"Come on. A blast of pure truth. You'll probably never see me again so use this as an opportunity to say what you've always wanted to say." Kate looked slightly bemused as Jack cajoled her. "Tell you what, I'll do mine too. What's the worst that could happen? I'll show you mine if you show me yours . . . "

"Really?" said Kate, in mock exasperation. "Are we going to play doctors and nurses as well?"

"Let's not get ahead of ourselves," cautioned Jack. "I might not like your profile."

"Just shut up and give me some of that paper," relented Kate. *Perhaps it will help to write it down. A different way of thinking it through.* "If we're going to do this, let's do it properly. Some quiet so I can write something down, then we can share and get it over with."

They sat in silence for a while, writing or staring out of the window, pens poised between teeth, lost in thought. Occasionally one of them would catch the other's eye and they'd smile, look away, and return to the task in hand. Kate's page filled up quickly, thoughts spilling out from her, whereas Jack doodled and dawdled, scratching out halting sentences before he had finished them. As he put a line through another false start he tossed his pen back onto the table and announced that he was going to get a coffee. Kate shook her head when he asked if she wanted anything.

Jack made his way along the carriage towards the buffet car, absentmindedly tapping the tops of seats as he passed until he inadvertently brushed against someone's head. Muttering an apology, he quickened his step and concentrated on the task at hand. She was distracting. In a good way. Why had he suggested this ridiculous game of *Let's reveal our true selves*? There was a reason his profile description was so ordinary: he was ordinary. Now she was going to find that out, to scratch below the surface and discover that there's only surface. Should have just kept it light and seen what happened.

Jack bought his coffee, returned to his seat and started emptying sugar into his cup. "We don't have to do this if you don't want to," he said to Kate, noting that she had now filled most of her paper.

"No, I'm ready. No backing out now." Kate grinned at him and snatched up what she'd written, eager to get going. *What the hell. Maybe it will be liberating. Maybe it'll just be a bit of fun to pass the time while we are delayed but, either way, like he said, we won't see each other again so what does it matter?* "Let's start with this. I have a tattoo. It's a butterfly in the small of my back. It'll sound corny but it was supposed to be a reminder to myself that beauty can be transient and fleeting – a reminder to appreciate things whilst they're here. Not many people get to see it but occasionally, if it's accidentally on show, I catch them looking at it and then I find myself wondering if they're just checking out my arse." She looked pointedly at Jack, who had the grace to look sheepish.

"You have a great tattoo," he offered. "And I thought everyone said *ass* these days anyway?"

Kate raised her eyebrows in mild rebuke before gesturing back at her paper. "Shall I continue?"

"Please do," said Jack. "I won't say another word."

"Particularly about my very British *arse*," said Kate. "An ass is a donkey you great . . . "

"Donkey?" offered Jack.

"Yes, you great donkey," agreed Kate. "*Baudet.*"

"Baudet?"

"Oh, sorry. It's donkey in French. I do that sometimes. Must

203

still be half-there, I guess. So, you really want to carry on with this?" Kate looked down again at what she'd written and Jack nodded his assent so she continued. "I'm pretty smart. I know, I know. I guess no one 'fesses up to being stupid on one of these profiles, but I'm really not. Straight-A student. Double first at Cambridge in Modern and Medieval Languages. Pretty smart and yet on my way back to my parents'. I quit my job at the Louvre. Imagine that. Imagine spending three years studying French and a year studying Art History and then getting a job at the Louvre. Well I had that, but I quit and now I've got no idea what I'm doing. I've got nothing to go home for, and I don't know what I want to do." Kate paused, looking again at what she'd been writing for the past twenty minutes. "I didn't write all that you know."

"What did you write?" asked Jack.

"I just wrote 'pretty smart but pretty stupid'," said Kate.

"I don't think it's stupid to be unsure," said Jack. "I think you're allowed some time to figure it out."

Kate shrugged and looked back at her paper. "Perhaps. It just seemed easier before, I guess."

Jack tilted his head, listening. "Before?"

"You know. School. College . . . "

"Ah I see," said Jack. "Before real life, you mean?"

Kate laughed. "Exactly. It was easier. It felt like a series of clearly marked destinations." She paused, flipped her paper over and drew a circle on the blank page. "Here, your next stop is GCSEs, and here," she sketched a straight line to another circle, "A-levels and on and on." She continued the line, idly tracing more circles along its trajectory, until stopping in the middle of the page. "Then what?"

"Look at all the blank paper," said Jack. "Exciting."

"It's terrifying," Kate retorted. "There's no lines. No predetermined destinations."

"I think it's OK to get a little lost for a while. Explore," said

Jack. "You're super smart – in two languages – so what if you don't know what to do with your life?"

"*Oui. Nous ne savons pas ce que nous voulons, et pourtant nous sommes responsables de ce que nous sommes – qui est le fait.*"

"I'll have to take your word for it – though I think I need to know more if I'm going to choose your profile, by the way. Particularly if I can't always understand what you're saying."

"Who said you'd get the chance to choose?"

"Humour me."

"I thought I was." Kate flipped her paper over and started to read again. "So this is me: I think too much and like to make plans. Sometimes I wonder what it'd be like to be a little more spontaneous."

"Swapping pretend dating profiles with a complete stranger on a train seems pretty spontaneous," suggested Jack.

"It's pretty something," said Kate. "Maybe *unhinged* would be a better word for it."

"There's a fine line between spontaneous and crazy, I guess."

"So it seems. What does yours say anyway?"

"You're not finished," protested Jack.

"I'm being spontaneous. Tell me a bit about you and then I'll finish mine."

"OK," shrugged Jack with a grin. "But be gentle with me. I'm not used to baring my soul like this."

"I bet you say that to all the girls."

Jack picked up his paper with a dramatic flourish and made an exaggerated point of clearing his throat. It was all *show* before he felt ready to *tell*. He was nervous for the first time since they'd started talking. He began reading what he'd written – some stuff about films he liked, music he listened to, books he'd read – before putting his paper down again.

"You know what? Like I said earlier, words aren't really my thing. Not written down at least. I could sit here and tell you about the things I love but they're all just another mask, aren't they? Borrowed identity. Just a different kind of way of telling people what they might want to hear."

"So tell me about you without that stuff," said Kate. "I really want to know."

"There's really not that much to tell. Maybe that's why I just churned out a list of cool-sounding stuff, so you can make a judgement about me based on the things I like, not the things I do or the person I am." Jack frowned and pressed his palms against his temples, rubbing at his head as if the action would smooth out the creases on his brow. "I don't know why this is so hard. It's just kind of mundane, I guess. I like to draw. No, scratch that. I *love* to draw. It's all I've ever really wanted to do since I was a kid. I used to fill up pages and pages of sketches and pictures." He gestured at the pad in front of him. "Now I carry a notebook round but never put anything in it. The odd doodle, but nothing that means anything to me anymore."

"So tell me about that. Why'd you stop?"

"My dad used to say *The only thing you should be worrying about drawing is your pension . . . and those scribbles won't give you one of those*. That was the sum total of his advice to me. All the time, growing up, he made me feel it was worthless, wanted me to get a 'proper job'. I don't really blame him, you know? He was just trying to look out for me in the way he thought best but it just killed the spark in me that made me want to draw. Didn't seem like there was a reason to do it anymore. You know what the worst of it is?" Kate shook her head. "The worst of it was that I let it happen, let that part of me go and just stopped. Studied to become a tax accountant instead. Don't judge me."

"Too late for that," replied Kate, gently. "Not about the accountancy thing, though. I was a tour guide in an art gallery so I'm not about to start throwing career choice stones from my ever-so-glass house."

"Glass pyramid," smiled Jack. "It's a big glass pyramid at the Louvre," he added, noting Kate's slightly quizzical look.

"Glass and metal, actually. Designed by I M Pei and consisting of 603 rhombus-shaped segments and 70 triangular ones . . . I can tell you anything you want to know about that pyramid. Its history, what it's for, that *Da Vinci Code* bullshit about it having 666 panes. I learned all this stuff by rote when I was there, churned it out to tick-list tourists on a daily basis, but I couldn't tell you how it made me feel anymore. None of it. The pyramid. The paintings. The sculpture."

"But you were doing what you loved," protested Jack. "Not like me."

"I thought I was," said Kate. "Somewhere along the way I forgot how to see things, I think. Forgot why I wanted to be there in the first place. A couple of weeks ago I found myself staring at *Diana of Versailles* . . . "

"Your co-workers had some pretty fancy names . . . "

"It's a statue, you arse. I love that piece. It's a depiction of Artemis . . . " Jack looked blank. "Artemis? No? Really? Looks like I've got some serious work to do educating you. She was the Greek goddess of the hunt. The Romans called her Diana and she was originally installed at the palace of Versailles."

"Hence the name."

"You're catching on. In the statue she looks so strong and sure, focused exactly on what she's doing. All poise and purpose. Pulling an arrow from the quiver on her back. It's what I'd describe to the tourists as a perfect marriage of form and function. Don't laugh, but I used to stare at pictures of her when I was studying and I found it . . . I don't know. I guess I found it inspiring. I wanted more than anything to see her for real and eventually I got to do that every day. But then, the other week, I was staring at the statue again and it was just a slab. Just cold stone."

"Maybe she just became too familiar? Like wallpaper?"

"I don't think it was that. Honestly? You wanted honest, right? Things went sour for me in Paris. No great drama I guess, not in the scheme of things. A relationship that went wrong and a life

207

that was built on being with him – his friends, his city, his flat. It felt like it was all falling apart. Somewhere along the way I forgot why I was there. I forgot about myself. Diana didn't change – I just stopped seeing myself in her anymore."

"I kind of get that," said Jack. "I stopped seeing myself as someone who drew. I forgot about chasing that thing I loved and built my life on all that advice my dad gave me. Made something of myself. But you lose something when you follow a track someone else lays down for you."

The tannoy interrupted them.

**We apologise for the delay. The broken-down train has just been moved out of Huntingdon station. Due to the length of time we have been stationary, we will be making an unscheduled stop at Huntingdon. Any passengers wishing to alight there should prepare to do so.**

Jack sat up straight in his seat and leaned forward. "Let's get off the train, go for a drink."

"Woah there, crazy man. What are you talking about?"

"Come on Kate. Live a little. Do something that wasn't in the plan." Jack laughed and sank back into his seat. "I'm done with staying on track for a while. I'm going to see what Huntingdon has to offer. I know it's not exactly Paris but it'll be fun."

"You're kidding, right?"

"No, I'm serious. You and me. I'd love to keep talking to you. It'll be like . . . like . . . " He tilted his head and looked up at the ceiling, searching for some filed-away information. "What was that film where two people got off a train and spent the night walking round some city?"

"*Before Sunrise*? *Sunset*? One of those," answered Kate. "Ethan Hawke. Julie Delpy. But you know the city was *Paris*, though. Or Vienna. I forget, but either way I'm not sure it would have been made if they'd decided to grab a drink in

208

Huntingdon." She shook her head, smiling. "I'm no one's idea of Julie Delpy either."

"I bet you are. Back when you used to think you were Diana of whatsit . . . "

"Versailles."

"Diana of Versailles. Form and function. Poise and purpose. I bet you still are like that. Anyway I'm no Ethan Hawke," conceded Jack. "But you know what? That's not the point. It doesn't matter where it is or who we're not. It matters who we are. Who we might be. And you don't get to find that out by spending your life sitting on a train with a fixed destination. Sometimes you need to get off and change the journey."

"You're pretty pleased with that metaphor, aren't you?"

"Not bad for someone who's not good with words," said Jack.

Kate shook her head again, still smiling at him despite herself. She stood up, away from the table, and made an excuse, told him she needed to use the ladies'. In truth she needed a moment to draw breath. Jack's offer had caught her by surprise; she was flattered and excited. There was an honesty about him that she was drawn to, but it scared her. It had been only a couple of months since things had imploded with François, a terse exchange on the Metro at Invalides after she'd found the messages on his phone and it was all over. Broken at Invalides. The irony hadn't escaped her. On their first date after that night they'd met he'd taken her to the Sacré-Cœur at sunset and they'd stood on the steps, looking across the city. It had been just how she'd imagined it, just how she'd assumed it would go when she moved to Paris, and it had all been a lie.

The toilet at the end of the carriage was out of order so Kate moved on, in to the first-class carriage beyond. She slipped into the cubicle and closed the door. The seat was down and she sat on it resting her head in her hands, elbows on knees, and began to cry. From laughter in the city of lights to sobbing on a delayed train in the space of six wasted months. From a first class degree to a first class job to a first class toilet. Kate tore off a piece of tissue and dabbed her eyes, watched as her tears soaked into the paper. At least she hadn't bothered with mascara today so she wouldn't end up looking like one of those imagined profile pictures Jack had been talking about earlier. What was it he'd said? *Smudged and dishevelled*? That felt about right. Her thoughts strayed back to him and she smiled sadly. Why did she have to meet him now, before she'd had time to work out what she wanted. Not now. Not when she'd walked away from what she'd spent years thinking she wanted. All that work. All those plans. She needed to think, needed a new plan.

Jack stood up and shuffled out to the aisle as the train slowed on its approach to Huntingdon. He pushed his phone into the pocket of his jeans and leant back over the table to pick up his sketch book. Kate watched him.

"It was really good to meet you," said Jack, extending his hand slightly awkwardly. "Are you sure you don't want that walk round Huntingdon? Or a drink?"

Kate took his hand, met his firm grip with her own and shook her head gently. "I'm sorry Jack. I just don't think I can right now. Plan was to get back home and you know I do like a plan . . . " Her voice tailed off and she shrugged apologetically. "It was lovely to meet you too though. Really, it was."

"By the way, that thing you said earlier, in French? I liked hearing you speak like that. What did it mean?"

"Oh that," answered Kate. "It means 'We do not know what we want and yet we are responsible for what we are – that is the fact.' It's Sartre. Told you I think too much."

"Deep," grinned Jack. "Listen, for what it's worth, I think that what you are is working out just fine. Don't worry so much about what you want. Try some stuff, see what happens. Like

I said, good to meet you Kate." He smiled at her, turned and made his way up the carriage to the doors. The train slowed, edging along the platform, and Kate pulled her gaze away from his retreating back and down to the table. He'd left his profile behind, a single piece of paper covered in his small, spidery handwriting. Kate picked it up with a rueful smile, turning it over in her hands. On the back was a drawing. In deft, firm pen strokes Jack had sketched her face. She was smiling and a shower of butterflies surrounded her head. Underneath it he'd written 'Don't leave reminders to yourself where you can't see them, life is fleeting, don't forget.'

The tannoy crackled again.

> **This is Huntingdon. Will passengers leaving the train here please make sure they have all their belongings with them.**

Jack had taken a couple of strides away from the train when he heard a bang behind him and the hiss of a door opening. He looked back over his shoulder and saw that someone had wedged their bag into the gap as the door was closing.

"You didn't get the butterflies right," said Kate as she stepped down onto the platform.

"Well I didn't get to look at it for very long," replied Jack, hurrying to help with her bag.

"Don't get any ideas, mister. Let's just start with that drink."

# End of the line
## by Lesley Close

*I've always loved trains. After the accident, I hoped that love would stay with me but now I realise the delight I've felt since I was a child has died. I no longer feel a thrill of excitement when I look out of the cab window and see the rail snake and vanish under the train. He made sure of that as his body hit the front of the cab and he died before my eyes. Did he really think it was only his life he'd end that day?*

I T was yesterday when Nate woke up, last night at least. 23:53. The gentle, steady glow of the digits illuminated the room just enough for him to see his feet as he swung them out of bed and on to the floor. He got up because he knew he had to do *something* to prevent those hideous, intrusive memories filling his mind. Lying awake for any length of time inevitably led his thoughts on to subjects he must avoid if he was to get back to sleep quickly – and sleep was imperative. *A tired driver is a dangerous driver.*

But, as happened far too often these days, Nate failed in his quest for calm. As he got back into bed, he had a sudden flashback of being helped out of the locomotive cab after the accident. And it *was* an accident, despite the voice that whispered to his conscience *You killed a man.*

214

Nate was moodily, reluctantly awake when the alarm shrilled at eight that Thursday morning. He swore as he banged his finger on the off button, lack of sleep making him irritable, before he turned over and closed his eyes again. As he fell in to a fitful, disturbed slumber he realised, with anger and frustration, that he would probably never again arrive early for work.

In the past Nate was nearly always early for work because he'd loved his job. He'd loved trains and railways and spent all his working life *and* holidays on them, the familiar British network as well as the delights of foreign railways. He and Wendy had spent a week travelling from Toronto to Vancouver on their honeymoon. The thrill of the train dashing through the snowy Canadian landscapes more than compensated for Wendy's endless complaints that she would rather have been lying on a Spanish beach. The next year they spent a holiday in Switzerland so he could marvel at the sights from – but mainly the line travelled by – the Bernina Express. They had once flown to Stockholm and taken a thrilling, if disappointingly shabby, high-speed X 2000 service across Sweden to Gothenburg: the beautiful route included twisting waterside views for most of the way. For their last holiday together they had spent a week in Italy before travelling home on the Venice Simplon-Orient-Express with its delightful restored coaches, comfortable beds and excellent food.

But – and in sharp contrast to that luxury – Nate's favourite holiday had been the one he took the year after his divorce from Wendy. He flew to Delhi then took local train services to the starting point of the Kalka to Shimla railway. He'd always wanted to travel on one of the narrow-gauge lines built to take families of the British Raj up into the hills to escape the heat of the Indian summer, but Wendy wouldn't go anywhere near India. He had loved the heady sights and smells he'd encountered there, notices in indecipherable and fantastically convoluted local scripts alongside formal and antiquated Anglo-Indian wording, steam and spices floating side by side on the clear, cool mountain air, tiny crowded platforms where the colourful silk saris of passengers mixed with the clean white *dhoti* of the hard-working engineers.

The familiar sights and smells of the British railway system – that unique blend of lubricating oil and the high whiff of electrical arcing, the worn edges of metal cabinets revealing differently coloured painted layers – had been one of the things that had always given Nate a good feeling about his job. And, as he settled in the cab, he had always enjoyed anticipating the surprises the journey would bring. Every time he drove the East Coast Main Line, it was the same but different – he'd see a bridge being repainted, further work on a line-side housing development, cows in a field for the first time in spring. There was nearly always a change somewhere alongside, over or under the line. But the horrible, unwelcome surprise he could *not* have anticipated the last time he drove the line meant that he no longer expected to enjoy looking out for those changes. During his period of counselling, he had travelled in the cab with the counsellor and with his good friend Gordon as driver: all he had been able to think about was what he had seen the last time he'd been in that position.

*It was the memory of blood that most haunted me after the accident. There was no way I could have avoided hitting that man. It takes a mile and a quarter to stop a train travelling at 125 miles an hour, and he stepped on to the track when the train I was driving was only a few hundred yards away from him. He knew what he was doing that day. He clearly wanted to die but, like every other person who steps in front of a train, he cannot have considered the effect his decision would have on the driver or on the many other people who would be involved in the clear-up and investigation. Some of the stories I heard in counselling – well, you wouldn't want to have those memories. It's no wonder some drivers are forced to give up the job they love.*

After that first journey in the cab, with Gordon at the controls, they had gone out for a drink. "You must be absolutely certain that you're ready to return to work," Gordon had cautioned Nate. He had been through a similar experience some years earlier and Nate knew Gordon thought he was being honest, considerate and caring when he said, "I took a lot longer than you just to get back in the cab. Don't rush it, Nate." But Nate felt he was made of stronger stuff than some of the drivers who had left the service – stronger even than some who *had* returned to work. He wasn't going to give up on the railways that easily, he wasn't going to let the love of his life be taken away from him without a fight. Nate knew that 'his' suicide-by-train was one of 279 last year and he felt certain that it could never happen to him again. *Could it?* Was that certainty enough to keep the love alive?

Recently, he had begun to consider the possibility that his love of the job *had* been destroyed by the appalling incident that led to his taking extended sick leave. He'd spent over a week at home, alone, before attending regular group therapy and counselling sessions for the next three months. He'd ridden in the cab with Gordon and the counsellor about four months after the accident, and had been the only person in the cab with Gordon about a week after that. The train operating companies and Network Rail offered counselling and therapy to all of the far-too-many drivers who, every year, were involved in the nightmare-inducing experience of having someone commit suicide by stepping or jumping in front of their train.

Apart from healing the hurt, if possible, it was the cost of losing drivers and having to replace them that led to the service being created.

> *The counselling helped. I was eased back in to the driver's seat with support and a phased return, all textbook stuff. But did I really accept the possibility that my future might not include driving trains for a living? I have spent all my time since the accident working toward today, and it had to come at some point. Today, when I have to drive the same route alone for the first time since . . .*
>
> *Who was I trying to fool when I reassured the bosses I was ready to come back to work? I was desperate to get back in the cab, but was I just kidding myself? I wish I'd listened to Gordon. Maybe he was right and I'm not ready to be in control on my own just yet.*

Nate knew how lucky he had been to have a job he had enjoyed so much. Wendy had hated her job working for the district council but it was 'secure and handy', as she often said. But while Nate was revelling in his fulfilling geekiness, Wendy was less than satisfied with her lot. The rather suave junior executive, who habitually gave her the eye on her daily rail commute, proved a lot more absorbing than Nate and soon absorbed her altogether.

Nate wasn't really surprised. They'd been growing apart for a while and Wendy's appreciation of all things rail-oriented was limited when they met and got more limited by the year. Nate knew it was ironic that a train took her away from him in the end, but even that couldn't diminish his love for the steel wheels. No: the horror of the accident and his growing alienation from the railway divorced him from the job he'd loved in a parting that was far more cruel and painful than his failed marriage.

*I can remember the look on his face, although I think
I must have closed my eyes almost as soon as I was able to
see it. I was braking like crazy, of course, but there was no
magic wand I could wave to stop the unbearable tragedy
that was about to take place. When I opened my eyes, a
moment later, there was a sickening mess on the windscreen
and the side window, and the train was coming to a halt.
I heard screaming, and realised it was me.*

Nate was glad that today's shift was mercifully short. His
only job was to take the 15:08 from King's Cross to York, then
return on the 18:02. He had some reservations about the future
now that Virgin/Stagecoach owned the service, but he knew
that fact wouldn't stop him doing his job. *What a sad phrase to
use*, he thought, *doing my job*. He'd never seen it like that before
but he knew that was all it was going to be in the future, trying
to do his job competently rather than driving a train because
he loved everything about it.

All the members of the train staff were present – and early
passengers settling in to their seats – by the time Nate started
his walk to reach the driver's cab. Jane, the train manager,
waved cheerily and called out to him as he passed. "Hi Nate –
welcome back! By the way, the third loo's out of action."

The gruff edge to his voice when he replied made Nate
realise that he hadn't spoken to anyone for a while. "There
are plenty of other lavatories on the train, so it should be OK."
The abrupt tone of his words startled Jane, who contrasted his
manner to that of the joyful, smiling Nate of old.

Nate felt great disappointment in his unfriendly retort to
Jane's innocent words of welcome. That attitude was new to
him, as was his regret that he now only felt like a *functioning* train
driver. He wasn't even sure at what level he was functioning.
Was his confidence in being able to return to the rails based on
external reality or internal hope? Was he returning to work

simply to avoid spending another lonely day at home? Was he just trying to escape his memories by escaping from the flat? He needed to try rekindling the love that had previously got him out of bed for work in a happy frame of mind before he lost touch with happiness altogether.

The HST was already ticking over so Nate checked the instrument panel and robotically observed that everything appeared to be working correctly. He failed to apologise for his earlier manner when he tonelessly spoke on the intercom to Jane, just to make sure that they could exchange communications, then he looked at his watch. Still a few minutes to go. Even with the locomotive just sitting in the station, he felt nervous, anxious, lonely. He tried to calm his breathing in an attempt to calm his mind. He'd never felt alone in the cab before that day, before he heard himself screaming and saw blood on the windows. Now he thought he'd feel alone even with someone alongside him . . .

Staring at the red light ahead, he could never remember a time when its STOP message had ever felt so personal. When it turned green and he got the platform guard's confirmatory signal to leave the station, he accelerated the locomotive away from King's Cross station towards York. He wished he felt more pleasure in the prospect, less dread. He just knew he had to carry on working. He had thought he would be able to cope: he had tried – successfully, he thought – to hide his fear and disappointment from everyone. But he had failed to hide it deeply enough to keep it from himself and he felt a rising tide of fear-induced bile burning his throat, starting to restrict his breathing.

As the journey proceeded Nate tried to ignore his body and mind and, instead, to devote his attention to the tasks that were required of him. Even before that awful incident, he had kept a careful lookout for people on or near the track ahead but now he was obsessed by it.

He observed the nearest signal aspect carefully and watched out for those ahead. He kept an eye on the weather – it was dry at the start of the journey but he would need to modify his driving technique if it started raining as the rails could become slippery.

Nate had never been able to remember whether the little boy who jumped into the air whilst on a fast-moving train in a maths (or was it physics?) problem would land where he took off or somewhere else. Trying to work out the logic of railway-related things like that had once delighted him, but it all seemed so trite now. Some deep part of his psyche knew that he would never again take any pleasure in the job, and that bleak prospect meant he was seriously considering his alternatives. The problem was his age – at forty-eight, he thought, he was probably too old to re-train. That unintentional pun smarted, and he tried to imagine what else he could do to earn a living. Maybe he should just sell the flat and downsize. If he moved far enough away from London he could buy a property without a mortgage, entirely possible after selling at current city prices, and get a job in a DIY superstore or a similar but utterly different environment. But he knew he'd miss the railway.

Nate looked round the familiar cab, wondering how much of his current sensation of being so ill at ease in the job was down to driving the route on which the accident occurred – and remembering the details? Maybe he should apply to work for a different train-operating company. How would that feel? He'd have to learn a new route, to start with . . .

On this East Coast line, Nate's many years' experience of working the route after memorising the 'manual' meant that he could tell exactly where the train was at all times. He knew he would never forget the details of this line, even if he did work another route. He imagined London cabbies must feel the same way about *The Knowledge*, ending up with a complete overview and full understanding thanks to a series of landmarks to guide their way. Nate never needed to read the mileposts as they went by – he knew where the train was by the topography and surroundings. After all these years driving the same route, he felt it in his body as an almost physical map and it came to mind like an endless narrow strip of bright steel with engravings marking the stations, bridges and trackside buildings. From conversations with musicians, he knew that they didn't need the sheet music in front of them because they could almost 'see' an overview of the printed score – with all its bars, slurs, ties, accidentals and so on – as they performed. His railway knowledge was the same sort of thing and he still loved that intimacy and total, reassuring familiarity: how much would he miss that if he got out of the industry altogether?

*"The memories probably won't go away," the counsellor had said, "but their intensity might lessen." She said that, if I wanted to get back in to the driver's seat, I had to find a way of dealing with thoughts about the accident for the rest of my life. I figured taking up the train-operating company's offer of a ride in the cab with the counsellor beside me would be enough to help me finally come to terms with the memories. But when I got into that familiar environment I was really surprised by my reaction. As I said, I've always loved trains and it felt very strange to find myself having such unwelcome and negative thoughts about being there. The counsellor told me that was a common reaction to incidents of suicide on the rails.*

As the locomotive passed yet another green signal, Nate glanced at his watch: 15:28. The service was running on time for the first stop at Stevenage, twenty-two minutes into the journey. He made the necessary preparations and brought the train to a halt in the right place.

During his time off work Nate had missed the music of the railways, the rhythm of the wheels crossing the points. That working symphony was essential, unavoidable, like the job's heartbeat. During this brief pause in the song of the rails, he opened the cab window to listen for the platform guard's whistle, and heard instead a blackbird singing. He saw it sitting on the fence at the end of the platform, a real free spirit, and he envied its ability to fly away, unfettered, at the first sign of trouble.

During the station stop, everything happened as it should. The train manager did her job of getting people off and on the train safely and quickly. As Nate heard the whistle and saw the dispatch bat held up to indicate that it was safe to leave the station, he wished he was looking forward to the next twenty-nine minutes until the service reached Peterborough.

Those uninterrupted stretches of pure train driving were among the things that once made Nate certain that he could not work in another industry. He used to love his job so much – beautiful landscapes, a well-maintained locomotive performing at its best and the prospect of the return journey. But now? Now he felt nothing but dread and anxiety at being alone at the controls of the locomotive, and he was filled with anger and frustration that he was *afraid* for the first time in his working life.

Today he would only have a short break at York before taking the same train back to King's Cross, arriving at 20:25. That service followed the same pattern of stops, so he would have this long stretch of station-free driving all over again. Of course it would be dark soon after the return journey started so he wouldn't be able to see the surrounding landscape, but he'd still know where he was at all times.

*I wish these negative, harrowing thoughts would lessen. Today I feel that my future cannot contain train driving, maybe not at all and certainly not on this line – the prospect is just too grim, too stressful.*

As the journey progressed, Nate sensed the approach of the level crossing at Offord Cluny where the incident happened. On the surface of the steel in his mind the crossing stood out, way ahead, like the opposite of a lighthouse. It was an approaching dark place, somehow way more prominent than the rest of those mental landmarks. And today he really dreaded seeing it.

Just knowing that the crossing was coming up, Nate felt the all-too-familiar tension of a panic attack developing. *No! Not here. Not at the controls!* He tried to calm his breathing to prevent his hands becoming rigid, useless. He'd never had a panic attack before the accident. He thought the counselling had provided the tools to stop them happening. He was hopeful that the counselling had worked – that's why he'd agreed to take this shift today . . . But hope is not certainty and in this case, Nate felt, hope is like looking for light in an endless tunnel of utter darkness. *Another painful railway analogy*, he winced.

The signals had been green for most of the journey and, as he slowed slightly for the Offord Curves, Nate saw double yellow lights ahead. Knowing that the signal might be followed by a single yellow then a red, he forced himself to relax and to slow the train a little more.

The next signal *was* that precursor to red. Before the accident the sight of a single yellow would have been the trigger to apply full service braking. But today something else provided a very different sort of trigger, his bleak frame of mind and a rising feeling of anxiety contributing to a serious and uncharacteristic lapse.

Nate saw a man with a dog standing by the Offord crossing and memories came flooding back into his mind, shocking, unwanted memories of blood and trauma and horror and deep, deep sadness. How had he allowed himself to hope that he would ever forget that day? That fateful day when he had seen a man and his dog step off the footpath and on to the track by Offord church, just south of the level crossing, the man running across the rails, pulling the reluctant dog behind him. He remembered seeing the two of them standing in the middle of the track for a moment before the man let go of the dog's lead. Nate was told, a few days after the accident, that the collie had been found by another dog walker, cold, wet and whimpering in a field beside the track a few hundred yards away from the gory accident scene. Hearing that news, Nate remembered his own instinctive reaction of wanting to run away from the train, from the crossing, from the horrifying mess and from the possibility that he would ever again have to encounter such a sight.

At the inquest it was revealed that the man, with his faithful dog, had been seen near the crossing several times in the preceding weeks. CCTV footage showed him taking notes which turned out to be details of train times, types, speeds. A letter he left for his GP made it clear that he had planned his suicide very carefully – he was dying of cancer and was full of dread at the prospect of suffering intolerably at the end of his life. The local papers reported his friends' shock when they read the letters he left for them, letters full of warmth and love but saying that he had no other choice. There was no doubt that he had intended to end his life, but Nate wished there had been some other and more dignified way he could have died.

Lost in those terrible memories, just for a second, Nate forgets about the possibility of a red signal ahead. A train slowing down from 125 miles an hour travels a long way in a second . . .

He brought his attention back to the moment and – damn! The signal was red. He had to apply the brakes much harder than should have been necessary. As the train came to a juddering halt, he was appalled at himself. Despite his ambivalence towards the job, he retained enough responsibility – perhaps still even felt enough pride – to be disappointed and angry at what any driver would see as a professional failure. He looked at his watch as an instinctive reaction to stopping at a red, trying again to calm his breathing and to relax. He remembered the counsellor giving him pointers to help with situations like this. *The memories will never go away*, she'd said. *You just have to find a way to live with them.* Nate had thought he *had* found a way to cope, to live with that intolerable intrusion into his peace of mind and love of his job, but the way he had felt since waking this morning made him wonder . . .

After sitting for two minutes with his eyes closed, trying to picture the *happy place* the counsellor had told him to go to at times like this, Nate felt calm enough to pick up the cab phone. The Network Rail operator told him that there was a broken-down train just south of Huntingdon station, on the crossover section before the platforms. Nate retained just enough self-control to relay that information to Jane, the train manager. Feeling the tension building within himself and needing fresh air, he opened the window. He heard a dog bark and saw the man who had been waiting to cross at Offord Cluny walking through the ploughed fields alongside the River Ouse.

※※※※※※※

Sitting doing nothing, feeling anxious and trying to stop dwelling on those memories, Nate looked around the cab in an attempt to follow another piece of advice from the counsellor: *Take your mind off it*, she had said. He saw his newspaper and reflected on how much he had once enjoyed completing crosswords during delays like this, as well as before and between journeys. Now he only associated them with the cab of a train, and all the joy had gone out of them.

In the therapy sessions Nate had heard some awful, harrowing stories. Many of the incidents ended in death but, far worse, many stories were about people who had suffered life-changing – but not fatal – injuries after stepping in front of a train, apparently intent on suicide. Nate felt it must be almost impossible for the suicidal person and their family to cope if they failed in their attempt to die but, instead, ended up brain-damaged or in a persistent vegetative state, especially if a terminal illness had driven them to take such desperate action in the first place. Compared to that 'outcome' Nate felt it was somehow almost selfish of a driver to struggle with the idea of going back to work, to find it hard to accept that someone's death or life-changing injury was the result of being hit by *your* train. "It wasn't your fault," the counsellor had reassured the therapy group members over and over again. "The suicidal person chose a train, not a driver. They had no idea who was at the controls, probably never even gave the driver any thought. The fact that *you* were the driver of that train on that day was entirely random." Nate had worked that out for himself early on, but it didn't really help him to cope.

Nate remembered hearing one of the drivers in the group therapy session confess that he had been reaching for his newspaper when *his* unforgettable incident occurred, just outside a station. Tears had stood in his eyes as he looked around the group, telling them that he had not been able to read with any pleasure since that day. Nate was glad that the driver had felt able to let the secret out and had vowed to make sure his newspaper was always out of reach if he got back into the cab. He knew that nobody would need to take any further action against *that* unfortunate driver – he was so traumatized by the events that followed his lapse that he would never drive a train again. Like Nate, he was in therapy to find his way back into the world of work but, unlike Nate, he would stay on the platform in future. In a sense that ex-driver was lucky – others had not been able to live with the memories of what had happened to them. *Maybe*, Nate thinks, *I should have taken that option too.* Falling out of love is very demoralising: it had happened to him twice and this second loss, of a love he had felt almost all his life, was so painful . . .

As the delay continues, Nate tries to concentrate on anything but the man with his dog. The image of him standing by the level crossing flashes across his mind over and over again, merging with images of that earlier, dreadful day into a gut-wrenching cocktail of memories.

As the delay continues, Nate finds it harder and harder to shake off the black mood which brings with it a sense of impending doom. He feels his muscles becoming rigid and his throat tightening; his breathing starts to become difficult. The claustrophobic cab, once so familiar and comforting, appears to be closing in on him. He feels that he must get out, he has to run away – from the train, from the memories, from his life . . .

The counsellor told him that, if things got really bad, one way to cope was to write things down. *Nobody ever needs to read what you write*, she emphasised. She had encouraged them to try it in one of their group sessions and Nate had found it helpful then. Maybe, if he can manage it, it will be useful now . . . Picking up his pen and notebook, he starts to write.

*I thought I could do this. I thought I could wipe those memories away and overcome the anxiety they induce. I thought I could carry on loving the railways and enjoying my job. But it's not working out like I'd hoped.*

*I wish I could still do this. I feel so cheated. One man wanted to die and he took me with him. I may as well be dead if I can't drive a train any more. Do I really want to give up the only job I've ever had, a job I thought I'd love for ever?*

*How can I get that love back? Can I get it back? Am I really going to let his death make me work in a shop? I hate the thought of being indoors all day, of having the same surroundings all the time. Where's the music of a job in a warehouse, apart from that tinny corporate radio they play all day? I'd rather die than do a different job.*

228

*What am I saying? I don't want to die, like the man with the dog did: dying would be an admission of defeat. I can't blame him. He didn't know me. He just picked a random train that would do the job he wanted. He wanted to die and I want to be a train driver who still enjoys his job. His dog lived – why can't I?*

Nate is looking at those final words, thinking about the man and dog he saw earlier and feeling the dark burden in his chest intensifying, when the telephone in the cab rings. It's the Network Rail incident supervisor with news that the broken-down train has been cleared and the track re-opened. Nate finds that he cannot speak – he feels breathless, panicky, trapped. He has tried really hard to overcome the trauma, to find a way to get back in to the job, but today's experience and his lapse of attention has tipped him over the edge. He slides off the seat, the phone in his hand, and manages to whisper *I can't do this anymore. Please help me . . .*

"Are you alright, mate? What's wrong?" Nate cannot answer the voice he hears. The silence from the cab is enough to spark a recovery operation: a relief driver sets off from Huntingdon, walking down the track to see whether Nate needs any help and, if necessary, to take the train into the station. As the train manager, Jane gets a call from the Incident Supervisor telling her what has happened and asking her to take responsibility for the train. She quickly makes her way to the driver's cab, unlocking it with the key she carries for just such an emergency.

Jane sees Nate lying on the floor, his breath shallow and gasping, and her first-aid training takes over. "Nate, can you hear me? What's wrong?" *At least he's conscious*, she thinks as he turns to look at her, his brow furrowed and sweaty, his eyes wide and staring. At first she cannot work out what's going on. "What's happened? Are you in pain?" she asks. She looks around but cannot see any evidence of what might have caused his collapse. Nate reaches for her hand, clutching it tightly as she tries to get him into a safe and comfortable position. "Is it your heart?" He doesn't answer, just looks at her with pain in his eyes. Jane puts her fingers on his wrist to check his pulse – it is racing, but regular. Finally, she recognises the symptoms of a panic attack. She knows there is little she can do to help him recover other than to stay with him and talk to him calmly – she cannot remove him to a place in which he will feel safe, for instance. She encourages him to slow and control his breathing, and radios to the buffet car for a cup of sweet tea.

Nate has a sensation of not being in the cab of the 15:08 from King's Cross to York. He isn't really sure where he is and everything feels unreal. By the time Jane sees the relief driver approaching, Nate looks a little better; his breathing is still faster than normal but he is speaking, albeit hoarsely and very quietly. His pulse is still racing and his hands are trembling. He is holding his tea, deforming the polystyrene cup between his rigid palms and spilling drops of the almost untasted drink. The relief driver is the first to speak, his brusque and confident tone a curiously welcome balm. "He OK to drive, d'you think?" Jane, still holding Nate's clammy hand, shakes her head.

The relief checks the indicator dials, then picks up the phone. "I dunno what's going on here," he tells the operator. "Everything looks OK with the loco. All looks fine, 'cept him. Reckon he needs a medic. We'd best get him off at Huntingdon. Can the service stop there?" He listens to the operator for a moment. "That's up to you. Can we call it" – he puts on a posh voice – "*an opportunity for passengers to use the facilities or to cross to the southbound platform* – summat like that?"

"What's your name, love?" the new driver asks Jane as he takes the seat Nate had tried so hard to re-occupy. Ignoring her answer, he carries on speaking. "OK, love, it's time to tell the passengers what's happening, about the extra stop. Just don't tell them the train's got a new driver. They'll take him off at Huntingdon and get him to hospital for a check-up."

As Nate is helped into a wheelchair, he glances along the length of the train. The realisation that he may have made his last rail journey as a driver hurts him deeply, but the current hurt – the tension and anxiety that are gripping his heart, his lungs, his power of reasoning – overwhelm any regret he might otherwise feel. A different driver is called for to take the train to York. As Nate is wheeled into the lift to cross the rails, he feels nothing but relief that he will never again run the risk of meeting someone intent on committing suicide on the railway and of being the means by which they bring a troubled life to an end. For the moment he doesn't care what his future holds as long as it excludes the horrifying possibility of someone bringing about their death at *his* hands, those of an innocent train driver.

With a lump in her throat, Jane watches Nate being wheeled away. *What does his future hold?* she wonders. She is brought back to the present and her own job by the distressed voice of a harassed mother, struggling to get a pram and a tetchy toddler out of the next carriage. Jane offers to help, then ruffles the lad's hair before looking along the platform. She is surprised to see how many other people have chosen to leave the train at this unscheduled stop.

While they wait for the replacement driver Jane sees a young man leave the train then turn and stand, staring back at it, with a dejected air about him. From the shelter of a doorway near the lift, a shifty-looking man is staring at a smartly dressed woman. She is deep in conversation with another woman who is, incongruously, wearing flip-flops. They appear to be exchanging phone numbers.

Jane's attention is drawn to the long queue outside the women's toilet. That could cause a problem: will they all get back on the train in time? She speaks to the new driver when he arrives on the platform, telling him that she must delay the train's departure until nobody is left in the queue.

After a further short delay, Jane is finally satisfied that everyone is back on the train. Just as she is about to blow the *Depart* signal on her whistle, she is irritated to see a case being thrust through the closing doors. *After this long delay? Really? You've only just made up your mind?* The doors automatically re-open and a pretty girl steps out. As Jane watches, the dejected young man rushes towards her and he smiles broadly as they walk off together. Despite her frustration, a feeling of warmth envelops her. *Love*, she thinks. *Love conquers all!* She is glad that, after Nate's loss of love, it appears to be young love that held up the train in the end.

# BIOGRAPHIES OF THE AUTHORS

**Liz Losty,** *Nemesis*
Liz was born in Belfast and graduated with a degree in Politics
from Queens University, Belfast. Liz travelled after graduating,
before settling in London and pursuing the well-worn path to
a career in the City. She now lives in Buckinghamshire with
her husband, three children and a guinea pig.

**Linda Cohen,** *Time to let go*
Linda was born in Leicestershire over 200 years ago.
An only child, she was educated (sort of) in Highgate. Linda
left school early due to a crisis in the family, and eventually
found someone in the City who took pity on her and offered
her a job as secretary. She spent the rest of her years regretting
her lack of schooling. Always a lover of creative writing, just
before leaving school she won the *Cadbury's Writing Competition*
for all schools (which is her only claim to fame). Married with
two children, and five grandchildren, she was inspired by
her eldest grandchild (who was in the middle of 'A' levels at
the time) to 'carry on learning – even now'! At a very young
age she was inspired by the Brontë sisters, and now reads
everything and anything. Linda worked as an estate agent
for many years before having a complete career change: she
trained as a social work assistant and worked on the spinal
injuries unit of The Royal National Orthopaedic Hospital until
she retired.

**Debbie Hunter,** *I'll be there*
Debbie was born and bred in Berkshire. At the tender age of
sixteen she emigrated with her family to South Africa where
she lived for thirty years. Although nostalgic for the heartbeat
of Africa she now considers herself extremely fortunate to be
living in Bucks where she enjoys the beautiful countryside.
She also appreciates the close proximity to London, where
her passion for all things royal and historical can be
accommodated.

**Angela Haward,** *Run rabbit run*
A native of Sussex, Angela has lived in Amersham for 26 years.
She is married with three adult children and a new grandson.
Following retirement, she is reinventing herself in her
original incarnation as a writer. After university, she worked
as an industrial journalist and did a bit of freelance work on
the side. She has had a few articles published and has also
produced a French teaching aid for primary school children.
In between, she has done a lot of other things – worked in
school business management, in PR work for a charity, set up
and run a children's second-hand clothes shop, travelled in her
motor home and cared for elderly family members. Angela is
privileged to have been part of Just Write who produced the
award-winning anthology *Spilling the Beans*. *Delayed Reaction*
is her second dip in to the fiction market and, here, she has
experimented with the thriller genre. The group has shifted
her faltering literary ambition into second gear!

**Chris Payne,** *Carpe diem*
Chris Payne moved to England from Canada in 1989 for
a year's work experience and never went back. Having
graduated with degrees in English Literature and Psychology,
she has been a journalist, an editor and a website manager
and now works in employee communications in the healthcare
industry. After several years in London she settled in
Amersham with her British husband and their three children
and they encouraged her to resume her youthful passion for
writing through Sally Norton's Just Write creative writing
group. Chris's favourite short story writer is Alice Munro.

**Emma Dark,** *In your own best interest*
Emma, born 1948, previously lived in Dorset and Surrey.
She has been a resident of Amersham for the past twenty years.
She is married with two grown up daughters. After retiring
Emma decided to follow her love of writing and is currently
trying to cope with her first novel, with which she has a
love-hate relationship. She has found the help and support
of her fellow creative writing students a great inspiration
to keep going.

**Richard Hopgood,** *Just in case*
Richard was born in 1952 in South East London, the son of a
policeman and a nurse and one of five children. After boarding
school in Sussex he studied English at Oxford and London.
His childhood ambition was to be a naturalist and a poet,
neither of which transpired. His favourite short story writer
is John McGahern.

**Vicky Trelinska,** *Facing the music*
Now that she has retired from careers as diverse as a freelance
musician and an officer in the Royal Naval Reserve, Vicky has
the time to concentrate on writing. Originally from Sussex she
was educated at St Swithun's School, Winchester, and trained
as a pianist at the Royal Academy of Music, London. So far
her writing successes include an article published in *Yours*
magazine, a story shortlisted in a *Writers' News* competition
and another shortlisted in *Writing Magazine's* subscribers'
competition as well as letters and press releases printed in local
papers. She is married to a retired GP and has a step-son.

**Phil Tysoe,** *Connection*
Faced with a mid-life crisis, Phil couldn't carry off a pony tail and didn't have the money for a Porsche so he decided to rekindle his early life love of writing instead. By day he works in the field of retail consumer insights and by night he watches too many HBO box sets, listens to a lot of Bruce Springsteen, and plays the guitar. Badly. He lives with his wife and daughter in Amersham.

**Lesley Close,** *End of the line*
Lesley was born in Oxford in 1956 and went to school in Buckingham. She is the youngest of three children and the mother of one. A voracious reader from an early age, Lesley somehow managed to avoid virtually all of the English-language literary classics until middle age! Her favourite writers include Ruth Rendell, Phillip Pullman, William Trevor and Alice Munro among (many) others. Lesley learned tap dancing and singing as an adult, and is a keen cyclist, walker and photographer. She has two non-fiction books in print and her third title, an e-publication, hit the 'shelves' in May 2013. She is continuing her very enjoyable research in to the life of a civil engineer who she hopes will be the subject of her next non-fiction book.

# DEDICATION

*Dedicated to The Royal Marsden Hospital, for the wonderful work they do.*

In support of

## About The Royal Marsden Cancer Charity

Every year The Royal Marsden provides treatment and care for more than 50,000 cancer patients and is at the forefront of cancer research. Its work influences how all cancer patients are treated and cared for, not just in its own hospitals but all over the world.

With the help of The Royal Marsden Cancer Charity, The Royal Marsden can continue to push the boundaries and benefit cancer patients, wherever they are.

The Royal Marsden Cancer Charity raises money to help The Royal Marsden provide world-class diagnosis, treatment and care for cancer patients, and supports the hospital's pioneering work in cancer research.

By supporting The Royal Marsden in this way the charity aims to make life better for people with cancer everywhere and strive for a future without it.